THE LEPER'S GARDEN
AND OTHER CONTAGIONS

JEFF CLULOW

THIRD EYE PRESS

This book is a work of fiction. Any resemblance to actual persons or events is coincidental.

Cover design by Jeff Clulow.

Cover images by Dan Cristian Păduret (Pexels) and Catsura Shichifuku (iStock). Rose photography by Pradit_Ph Pravet (iStock).

Cover fonts: Lightfoot by Paul Lloyd, EB Garamond by Georg Duffner. Interior fonts: EB Garamond and Cinzel by Natanael Gama.

Editors: Clare Rhoden, Brandi Hicks, Shelly Jarvis and Jodie Francis.

Proofread by Liz at Elizabeth Bird Proofreading Services.

Caution: this collection contains horror, gore and adult themes.

ISBN (ebook): 978-1-7641397-3-1

ISBN (paperback): 978-1-7641397-2-4

First Publication

Rats' Alley – first published in the anthology 'From The Waste Land' by PS Publishing (UK) in 2022. Edited by Clare Rhoden.

The Storytellers – first published in the anthology 'New Tales of Old – Volume II Wolves Among Us' by Black Ink Fiction (USA) in 2022. Edited by Brandi Hicks and Shelly Jarvis.

Unshadowed – first published in the anthology 'Penny Blood Tales' by Black Ink Fiction (USA) in 2023. Edited by Jodie Francis.

The Hare Bride – first published in the anthology 'Fantasy On Four Feet' by Black Ink Fiction (USA) in 2022. Edited by Clare Rhoden and Brandi Hicks.

Acknowledgements

MY THANKS goes first go to my patient family who endure the burden of my successes and failures in equal measure. Next I thank my friend, writer, editor and creative dynamo, Clare Rhoden, whose influence is evident in many of these stories. Clare, part of this book is you. And it's all the better for it. Thanks to the wonderful team at PS Publishing in the UK for publishing Rats' Alley, a story that later made the finals of the Aurealis Awards for best horror novella. Thanks also to Gemma Paul and Kate Campbell at Raven & Drake (UK) for accepting several of these tales into various anthologies and to Brandi Hicks and Shelly Lusk at Black Ink Fiction (USA) for the same. I thank each and every editor who has touched this collection and a special word of thanks to the ever-fastidious Liz at Elizabeth Bird Proofreading Services for the final spring clean of my manuscript. Gratitude also to my friends and fellow writers of dark fiction, Brent McGregor, Alister Hodge, Georgina Ballantine and David-Jack Fletcher. Your advice and suggestions for these stories are clear upon the page. A special note of thanks to Aveline Pérez de Vera for help with The Deceiver's Tale and a monumental *gracias* to Lino Pérez Fernandez for the daunting task of translating *Duranzo's Curse* into Spanish.

For Jo,

Lana

and Billie.

My triform knot.

CONTENTS

1

RATS’ ALLEY

Speak to me. Why do you never speak. Speak.
What are you thinking of? What thinking? What?
I never know what you are thinking. Think.
I think we are in rats' alley
Where the dead men lost their bones.
                    The Waste Land – T.S. Eliot

HE STILL SEES THEM in the dim, narrow places.

They wait for him in the passageways between streets, the laneways behind houses, the cut-throughs, tunnels and confined, echoing descents to the Metropolitan Line.

He passes, head down, avoiding eyes, his feet upon firm pavements and stair-treads; theirs still held by the clinging, sucking mud. Over the top of sandbags they peer, rifles at the ready, watching the space beyond the wire. Even the youngest faces among them are old with fatigue.

Once, he turned into an alley off Fleet Street. A soldier in a filth-caked uniform stood before him with an unlit cigarette upon his lips and an appeal for help in his eyes. Without thought, he reached into his pocket, found a box of matches and struck one. Looking up, he saw a woman and her young daughter at the other end of the alley. They watched him with wide eyes, hand in tightly-clasped hand. Then they turned and hurried away, leaving him offering a flame to the empty gloom.

The city is filled with sounds and sights that haunt. At night the street-lights are flares that drift over no-man's land, revealing targets of the wounded for enemy snipers. The electric trams that roll over Westminster Bridge from the southern suburbs give out their *clatter-clatter, clatter-clatter,* and become the sound of distant Vickers guns or German *maschinengewehr.* In the rough, unruly schoolboys raised without fathers, he sees the faces of those who lied about their age to the recruiting officers. Those mouths are stopped with mud now, their virgin cheeks never felt a razor. He will forever see the crops of bright hair, blond and gold, marking out their resting places in the cruel wire.

His discharge gratuity and ration book have grown thin. So have the soles of his demob shoes. Every day he paces the length of Fleet Street in search of work. *Have you tried Marshalls on Wardour? They do pamphlet work.* Yes, he has. It was they who sent him here. *Have you considered starting out with a smaller newspaper, a more local one?* I'm not starting out. I've worked the nationals in Fleet Street since I was a boy. *But don't you have any recent typesetting experience?* I've been fighting a war. *Yes, yes, well, if you were to gain some more current experience, we'd be happy to reconsider.*

He has returned home to find the world he fought to save

firmly in the grip of selfish old men once more. No parades. No celebration of victory. No thanks for services rendered.

'Well, what do you expect, Will?' says Alf, a friend from the same battalion. Alf speaks over the rim of his pint-glass in a cramped, smoky public house. 'A world war's been fought but the world won't learn from it.' Alf looks very different in peacetime, unrecognisable even. Is it the cloth cap he wears? It doesn't suit him, doesn't look right. 'And have you heard, they're going to raise a memorial to us,' continues Alf, 'smack bang in the middle of High Holborn, ten feet across and thirty feet high. I reckon the bloody thing'll hold up traffic for centuries.' He raises a hand in the tobacco-thick air to place the final words upon the imagined monument: 'The Royal Fusiliers. London Regiment.' Alf gives a chesty laugh. 'Here, if they put the names of the dead on it, we should go take a look, Will.'

'Why?'

'To check we aren't there. You never know!' Alf's laugh now becomes a coughing fit.

Will knows that if the monument was the length and breadth of Holborn, it still wouldn't be large enough to hold the names of the dead.

They say their goodbyes in the street outside. Will pictures Alf in his tin hat once more. Now he recognises his old friend, the grin that hides the fathom-deep fear. Over his shoulder he clutches the strap of his rifle. He turns from Will with a wink and walks into the night, over duckboards and between trench walls. Will hears his cheerful whistle long after he has vanished.

◄━━●━►

He decides to return his greatcoat. Among his discharge papers is a printed sheet of instructions. *£1 (one pound) is redeemable upon return of Military Greatcoat, property of the Government, at the railway station of your choice. Greatcoat must be cleaned and accompanied by completed form Z50.* The instructions are poorly printed. No typesetter worth his wage would let such plates see ink. The letters run up against each other and the lines are crammed too close. They should have used more lead. Why so little? Was it in short supply? Had it all been used up in the bullets they fired at each other?

He could do with the money, and he no longer wants the coat. He would never wear it. It's damaged, worn, and when he pulls it on, he pulls on feelings he no longer wishes to feel. Better that a seamstress does what she can with it and that it pass to some slap-faced recruit in Aldershot who will never wonder at its history. The instructions outline the cleaning process.

1. Brush the coat vigorously. In the small back yard, he attacks the coat with a stiff broom. Clods of soil from the Somme and Beaurevoir are worked free. Dust from Amiens rises in the late morning air. He sweeps everything into a dustpan and rests it on the lid of the bin awhile before tipping it away. This is what it had all been for: soil, dirt. A war of dust, yardage, territory and earth.

2. Wash coat in lukewarm water with mild detergent or bar soap. He fills the bath and lets the coat soak awhile. The water leeches tendrils of clay-brown from the fabric. Soon the bathtub is the bottom of a shell-hole, opaque with the milk-tea mud of Northern France. Under its surface lie the bodies of his countrymen.

He remembers wading through such shell-holes, stepping on

faces, feeling the crack of bones.

3. Rinse and roll to expel excess moisture. Dry flat. He lights the gas fire with a match, folds away the rug and places the coat on the floor. The room soon smells like a damp dugout: cigarettes, paraffin stoves, overflowing latrines.

The coat will likely take a week to dry, so he resumes his daily labour of combing Fleet Street for work. At Ludgate Circus a crowd has gathered to watch policemen arrest two Romany women. Their likely crime is selling lucky heather, or messages of comfort from the dead to the living. The elder of the two women kicks and spits curses at the policemen in the jagged, hack-throated language of her people. Then she catches Will's eye, and the fight leaves her. Fearful eyes remain upon him, and her fingers stab and stab the air in his direction to ward off evil.

Is he evil? He thinks he might be. No man can kill and call himself virtuous. Not in the name of God, not in the name of country. He knows now that the greatest hell of all is the one made by men. He's journeyed there and still feels its taint upon him, still feels the weight of its sin. Once, he believed goodness and truth sat at his shoulder and whispered in his ear, keeping him in the narrow way. Now, a demon scratches at his conscience and goads him to wickedness.

Amid the confusion, the younger of the two Romany women bolts, losing herself in the knot of onlookers. A policeman raises his whistle to his mouth and blows.

The sound strikes through Will's chest like a bayonet.

He is there once more, back at the place it began and ended: hurrying in fear through the support trenches under the bleak sky of an October dawn. The artillery bombardment has begun. The air shakes with the thunder of the guns. The NCOs spur the men along, herding them like frightened cattle through the crowded, narrow trenches – *take a left at the signpost for the forward OP, down Piccadilly, past Kitchener's (keep your head down), then into Zig-Zag trench...*

He knows what lies after Zig-Zag. It's the last trench of all. The firing line.

Rats' Alley.

Beyond that, there is nothing but the German guns.

At the head of Rats' Alley he stops, he does not know why. He finds himself staring at the battalion's makeshift place of worship. The Last Ditch Church. *The Chapel of the Sandbags.* A rough wooden cross is suspended in an expanse of barbed wire and camouflage netting that stretches across the trench wall. Wedding rings, lockets, photographs and letters from the dead hang there. *If you are reading this, then know I will not be coming home...* In other places hang the prayers of the faithful, or pledges and pleas for deliverance: *Spare me Lord and I'll let Meg make an honest man of me. Spare me God and I swear I'll make things right with my father...*

Nailed high above, painted in white on a palette of duckboards are the words of Psalm 91: the soldiers' psalm. Below, a chaplain kneels among a huddle of men in prayer.

Will feels inside his collar. His fingers close around the silver chain. He unhitches the clasp and pulls the small silver cross free. He finds a place on the wire and hangs the cross by its eye. Then he pulls a scrap of paper from his breast pocket and, with a blunt pencil, he begins to write.

Dear Lord...

The bombardment stops and he hears the shouts of men from distant trenches. The silence rings more loudly than the exploding of the shells. A lieutenant with an unholstered Webley checks his wristwatch and lifts a whistle to his lips. Then he blows.

The first detachment climbs from the trench into open ground. They make progress. Will counts the seconds: *one, two, three, four, five... A hundred feet? Maybe more?*

The enemy is either in recovery or they have been cunning, waiting for targets to fill their gunsights – waiting for the charge to reach a point of no return. Now the German guns sound out their *clatter-clatter, clatter-clatter.* The noise is close, deafening, murderous. In Rats' Alley, men close their eyes, raise fists to their brows or hang their heads. A minute later the guns rattle to a stop and all is silent once more.

'B company, fix bayonets!' screams another officer.

Will looks at the psalm, the sandbag altar, and the silver cross he has placed there.

Then he looks at the scrap of paper in his shaking hand and the words he has written.

Dear Lord...

'Are you alright, love? You look a bit peaky.' The woman's voice is close. Ludgate Circus floods back to him. The hubbub and sounds of traffic fill his hearing once more. He glances to his side, at a middle-aged woman in a too-youthful hat. Her expression is wrinkled with concern. He does not know how long he has stood there, lost to the present.

'I'm fine, really I am,' he says.

On Thursday he reads the *Evening Standard* and is intrigued to learn that playhouses and movie theatres are now offering free admission for returning soldiers. The newly-opened *Palais de Danse* in Hammersmith hosts Friday afternoon tea dances, free of charge. He visits a barber, puts on a good suit, and attends. The interior of the Palais is grand, decorated in the latest *chinoise* style with silk lanterns and carved, lacquered woodwork. A band plays upon the stage but their music is made inaudible by the heels of the vast throng of dancers that rotates over the boards of the dancefloor.

Clatter-clatter, clatter-clatter.

He commands his mind to hear nothing more than the sound of dancing, and collects his teacup. He makes his way to an empty table. Nearby, a girl, dark and very beautiful, sits like Penelope in Ithaca, beset by suitors. The men clamour round her, fingers tucked into jacket pockets, waving cigarettes in accompaniment to their witticisms. She endures them with a raised brow and both hands held flat over her dance card. One of them reaches to steal it and she stands, angry now, and marches from them. She spots Will at his table alone and sits beside him. Perhaps he is the lesser threat? The young men disperse in search of easier conquest. One of them bumps hard into Will's chair as he passes.

'Filthy, fucking toe-rags,' she says. Ugly words from such lovely lips. 'What's happened to all you men since the war? Did all the good ones cop it? Is that it? Is that why there's only shirkers and tosspots left?' She watches the dancefloor, jaw clenched. 'So what's your story?'

'My *story?*'

She studies him now with a sidelong look. 'Yeah, were you *over there?*' She nods towards an unfixed location in the cosmos.

'I was.'

'Then how'd you make it back in one piece?' It's an accusation.

He stands to leave and she covers his hand with hers. 'Sorry.' She smiles a little in apology. 'There's still a couple of spots on my card. They're yours if you want. For helping me out.'

In between her dances with other partners, he waits. Each time, she excuses herself and returns to the table, taking sanctuary in the chair beside him. They fall into conversation. Her name is Winnie. She likes Dixieland and Ragtime, Harold Lloyd and Pall Mall cigarettes. At some point before the last dance, she asks if he will walk her to the train station. He says he will. At this, her voice falls to a whisper and her dark eyes, as terrible as any oath, call him to confession. 'You are *intact?*' she asks.

He assures her that he is. He finds the question direct, base, although its implication kindles an even baser hope. The demon scratches.

'I won't take no damaged goods. I ain't shopping for seconds,' she declares.

He nods in official recognition of the warning.

They walk towards the station. This late in the year, the dark rolls in early. The air is hung with mist, as if a light rain has been frozen, mid-cascade. She announces she wants to see the river, and so they change direction, heading for Hammersmith Bridge. They stroll along the north bank in the misty lamplight, past Dutch barges and narrow-boats moored beside piers. To their landward, fading into the night, is a small, well-kept park. With excitement, she grasps his hand and hurries him towards a bandstand in the veiled dark. It rests on a plinth of hexagonal stone, with fluted columns of cast iron and a domed roof. Although open to the elements, it feels dry inside. They collide with each other, her mouth and nose crashing into his face. Mouth against mouth, breathing hard, hands under clothing. He has forgotten desire, forgotten its power, the force of its drive. He is in the demon's thrall now.

'Put your jacket on the floor', she whispers, 'quick.' He hurries to oblige and she pulls him down, raising skirts, raising knees. She lies upon his jacket on the stone flags and pulls him closer still. Strong fingers, sharp fingernails, sink into his back and he cries out – not a shriek, not a scream, but nonetheless a voiced reaction to his pain.

She is upright now, pushing him away. She draws her skirt back over her knees and sits sideways, apart from him. She's dug in. The bales of wire are drawn across, her eyes are fixed upon him like sentries. Then the first ranging shot. 'You lied,' she says.

'It's only mustard gas,' he explains.

'Told you I did, I won't take no damaged goods. I ain't shopping for seconds.'

'It will heal, in time,' he offers.

She stands and makes to leave but hooks a toe inside his jacket. She hops once, twice, then kicks it free and escapes down the stone steps of the bandstand. He watches her furious shape melt into the damp night. Perhaps tomorrow she will resume her shopping in the dancehalls of Leicester Square or Shaftesbury Avenue. She must know by now that London has only half the men it used to, and that those left, like him, will always carry signs of injury. He thinks she aims too high. She should lower her sights.

He gathers up his jacket, studying it. It is summer in France and he is hot. In his hand he holds his tunic. He hangs it on the hilt of a bayonet thrust into the sandbags, then hangs his webbing and water canteen over it. Stripped bare to the waist, he tilts his helmet against the sun and takes up his entrenching tool. He's part of a two-column detail tasked with digging observation trenches out into no-man's land, toward the enemy.

From a point behind the German line, a battery of *feldhaubitze* opens fire. The shells rake the air above them and land nearby. As one, the men throw themselves flat. But the explosion does not come. There is laughter among the men now, and mention of *duds*. Then comes the smell: burnt rubber, garlic, petrol. One of the men yells 'Gas!' but the windblown cloud of sulphurous yellow is already upon them, spilling into the trench. He drops his entrenching tool and runs back to his kit, breath held, eyes squinting. He tears off his helmet, pulls his box respirator from the webbing and covers his head. No time to throw his tunic over his shoulders or take up his rifle. He throws himself to the bottom of the trench as the poisonous tide flows over him. The acidic gas attacks the sweat on his back in an instant, burning, blistering, paring back the skin. He writhes face down, keeping the injury confined to his back. At the casualty clearing station a Welsh medical officer tells him he's done the right thing. His quick thinking has saved his lungs and eyes. With scissors they cut the blistered skin from his back and apply antiseptic. He'll be back at the front in days they tell him.

In that much they are right. Will returns to his post and his wounds heal for a time. But by the end of the war, the skin on his back opens up again. The effects of the gas on skin are considered temporary, so Will never complains lest he is branded a malingerer.

He never returns to the Palais in Hammersmith. In the *Evening Standard*, he reads of another new establishment offering free admission for returning soldiers: the Embassy Club on Old Bond Street. After handing in his greatcoat at Charing Cross station he attends an afternoon tea dance there. Unlike the Palais there are very few tables and seating is reserved for ladies and couples only. So he stands at the fringe of the crowded dancefloor, observing the slow, inexorable orbit of human courtship.

Clatter-clatter, clatter-clatter.

His attention is drawn to a table of young women who talk and laugh, conspicuous in their merriment. By the way they confide in each other, leaning close to whisper secrets, he picks them for good friends. One of their number excludes herself. She sits with downcast eyes, unlaughing, unsmiling, as if, in some temporal exchange she is the keeper of all their sorrow. Once their revelry is done, she will return their coats, hats, and sadness so they may resume the track of daily life.

As one, the laughing women rise to leave and he understands. She has not excluded herself. She is not one of them. She is alone.

As he makes his way to her, she fans herself with her dance card in general invitation. It's mechanical though, as if she'd rather be elsewhere, doing something else. She seems fragile, as if by a careless hand or an unkind word she might shatter like glass. He would not call her beautiful, yet there is beauty in her that draws him.

'I wonder if there are any spots left on your card?' he asks.

She looks at him as if receiving a fatal diagnosis. She coughs. 'There are,' she says. 'I can put you down for the foxtrot if you'd like.'

'I'd like that.'

Pen in hand, she hovers over the card 'Mister...?'

'Harper.' He notices that the dance card is largely blank. Against the names of the men that appear there she has written scores. *Fielding 3. Perkins 2.*

He retires to the fringe of the dancefloor once more and watches her. From time to time she lifts her eyes to search the room then, finding him, allows herself a tiny smile.

They dance the foxtrot. It's faster than he would like. He steps on her foot and is forced to stop. He counts them both in, nodding to the beat as dancers behind collide into them. She holds him gently, never looking up, and merely blushes at his clumsiness. He has not danced in a long time, he tells her. The line of her nose is perfectly straight.

He asks her for the two-step and the waltz. She agrees. At the interval he collects tea and sandwiches for them both. The crusts have been cut away in imitation of gentility, yet the fillings speak otherwise: corned beef, fish paste, boiled egg. They sit at the table as a couple among other couples and compliment the sandwiches. She tells him her name is Ada. She likes Tennyson, arum lilies and Debussy. She likes Southend in blustery weather when she can call the beach her own. She likes the gardens at Kew. *Has he been?* Not in a while. *They should go sometime.* He says he'd like to.

For all her friendliness, he senses her unhappiness. Could it be that the war has injured her too? At this, he feels a kind of comradeship with her. What has she lost? *Who* has she lost?

Where is your wound? How deep does it go? Does it still hurt?

He thinks he would like to help her heal. Perhaps she might do the same for him. The thought lifts him.

They leave together, to say their goodbyes in Old Bond Street. She places her dance card on the table and, while her back is turned, he takes an ungallant look. Despite his two left feet, she has awarded him a '9'.

In the street outside, the London evening shelters the parting couple under a starless sky. If all the constellations of the universe were visible, they would not have noticed. They make plans to meet the following week. A walk along the Embankment, then tea at the Winter Gardens.

Their dance continues: two souls holding each other in a swirling, clattering crowd. But the dance becomes more and more their own. With each meeting they fall into comfortable familiarity, their steps each anticipated by the other. They find their own tempo, become less clumsy, less like strangers. To the eyes of the world, although they cannot see it themselves, the floor is now theirs, and they dance as one.

◄—●—►

For many nights he sleeps even less than usual. The damp greatcoat is gone, but the dugout smell remains, dragging him down through the dark tunnels of his nightmare. Over and over he witnesses the same scenes, as if seeing them once was never enough. Ada is a part of these scenes now. Among the teeming of shouting, muddied men, she stands on the duckboards of the trench, bodies rolling at her feet. She wears a pretty dress the colour of bluebells and clutches the looped handles of her handbag. He removes his tunic, strips naked and bares his wounds for her. An end to secrets. With brimming eyes she shakes her head. He has burdened her too greatly. She shatters like glass, or runs from him, or else her dear face is disfigured by disdain and she sees a ploy in his actions: she thinks it is a scheme to draw out her pity.

He should have slept more soundly. She is stronger than she looks, and he should have trusted the height and breadth of her compassion. He tells her of the wound upon his back, that he is not the whole man she may have thought. He does not wish to deceive her. Ada's reply is to take his hand and tell him that he is more complete a man than any she has known.

Respectful of his confession, she now reveals her own wound. She has lost a brother, Lionel, at Jutland.

He feels her pain. And his own shame. Her wound runs deeper than his.

Lionel sits upon the writing bureau in her rented room. He smiles, healthy and steadfast from his silver frame, dressed in his naval uniform. By degree, Will learns how much of Ada's heart was filled by her brother, and how empty it has become to let him go. At night, Will often catches her standing by the bureau, whispering to the darkness.

In quiet moments while Ada reads or busies herself with their supper, Will and Lionel regard each other, eye to eye. At first there is reserve between them. Will believes they might have made good friends, so long as Lionel had not been too protective of his sister, too zealous in his scrutiny of her companions. He imagines the three of them together at Southend, or Kew, in a time that never knew war. One morning, while Ada sleeps, he makes a hushed promise to Lionel. He will try to love Ada as much as Lionel ever did. He will try, to the limit of his being, to lead her back to happiness. Lionel beams with ruddy vitality from his photograph. He seems happy with the proposal.

Ada waits for Will in the here and now, on park benches, in the nooks of tea shops or the window seats of cafés. She sits patiently while he drifts away to places unknown to her. When he returns, eyelids fluttering, she greets him with a troubled smile.

Where have you been my love?

She wants to take him to Kew, but the gardens will not bloom until spring, so they take a train to Hampton Court instead. The palace is closed from autumn until spring. They should have foreseen this. The grounds are overgrown with neglect. The gardeners are elsewhere now – planted in French soil perhaps. Rather than make a straight return to the city, the two of them stroll along avenues of ancient chestnut trees, arm in arm. They gaze into empty fountains, lament the unpruned roses and meander the unweeded pathways of the formal garden. Looking up with a gasp, she spots something, and steers him with girlish excitement.

From outside, the maze seems very large, with impenetrable box-hedges of clipped hornbeam. They study the map beside its entrance, trying to fix its twists and turns in their memory. She points to the map's centre. 'The Lovers' Temple,' she declares, eyes shining. 'Let's find it.'

She leads, pulling him by the arm. The interior of the maze is silent, dark. They hurry down narrow hallways of green, turning once, twice. A dead end. Retracing their steps, they try a different route. She pulls him along by the hand now. They turn another corner and he slows. Towards him, stretcher-bearers with filthy faces carry a near-dead man, torn apart by shrapnel. The men pass him with hollow, unblinking eyes. Ada leans close and kisses him. 'Come find me at the Temple,' she entreats him. Her hand slips from his and she is gone, rounding corners of densest green, trailing a laugh. He panics now and runs after her, through turn after turn, and into more dead-ends. He enters a straightway and is struck still. Before him, a procession of soldiers walks in single file: men with blistered faces and bandaged eyes, gas-blinded. They each hold the shoulder of the man in front to find their way. Pressed up against the hedge he lets them pass, then stumbles onward calling Ada's name. Over duckboards now, a rifle slung over his shoulder. The hedge of hornbeam has turned to mud. The sounds of artillery and screaming fill his ears. He turns the corner from *Zig-Zag*, and halts. *The Chapel of the Sandbags*. His silver cross gleams from the tangle of wire.

Ada finds him on his haunches. Head bowed, clutching his scalp, knuckles blanched. She kneels on the damp ground beside him and holds him until his shaking stops. 'When will you come home, Will?' she asks.

◄―●―►

Their lovemaking is gentle. She wants to see the scars upon his back.

She needs to know how best to avoid hurting him.

He removes his shirt and vest, revealing the long winding sheet of gauze around his torso and over his shoulders. It takes a full half-hour to remove the bandage without tearing the skin. When the gauze and dressing drop to the floor, Ada's hand goes to her mouth. 'I never knew,' she says. 'Why has it not healed, Will?'

'I don't know, and the doctors seem unclear. They talk of a secondary infection.'

She asks to accompany him on his next visit to the military hospital in Chelsea. She wants to understand. She wants to help. She is no nurse, but she can learn.

The doctors at Chelsea inspect Will's unhealed back. They make notes and mutter to each other. They are unwilling to answer Ada's questions or, it seems, entertain the presence of a woman, no matter her relation to their patient. The nurses are more sympathetic. They show her how to bathe the wound, dry it, and apply the antiseptic. They teach her how to dress and bandage it. 'Shouldn't this have healed by now?' she asks them.

'Yes,' they tell her. 'If this was caused by gas, it should have healed. But this looks less and less like mustard gas.'

In the days that follow, Ada grows distant, retreating deeper into concern for him. She studies Will's face at length but does not voice what she is thinking. He feels the weight of her worry and draws her out. 'What is it Ada? What's on your mind?'

She seems afraid to answer. 'If the Chelsea doctors cannot help, then we should seek out those who can.'

He sighs. 'With what? I have no money, no job and a Harley Street physician is beyond my means. There's no one to turn to.'

She looks away, gazing from her room's narrow window, to the sky beyond the washing lines and chimney pots. 'What if there were?' she murmurs.

'Such as who?'

She turns back to face him, taking a new course. 'Do you trust me?'

'Of course!'

'Enough to entertain a belief?'

'What kind of belief?'

'A belief in something – *other than ordinary*.'

'Go on.'

She wrings her hands. 'I have a cousin, Clara. She works as housekeeper in a small hotel in Euston. The position is piecework.'

He feels his eyebrows gather.

Ada continues. 'So, during the war, she supplemented her wage by other means. To look after her family.'

'What means?'

'She helps people, Will. She *heals* people.'

'She's a *healer*?'

'She is much more.' Ada's eyes flit around the room. 'She heals people in ways beyond the physical. She helps me with Lionel.'

'How?'

'We speak.'

'You and this – *Clara*?'

She looks down, shaking her head.

Will gets to his feet and paces the room. 'I don't need help from counterfeit spiritualists or table-rappers.'

Ada looks up at him now. Her eyes display the sheen of hurt.

He notices and reins in his derision. Kneeling in front of her, he takes her hands. 'Ada, a war has ended and there's a huge market in grief. There's money to be made from people's misery, that's all.'

'She has never asked me for money.'

'But there will always be those willing to take comfort from this kind of confidence trick.'

'She is my cousin. She'd never trick me.'

'But honestly, Ada, tea leaves and mumbo-jumbo?'

'Clara has no need of tea leaves. Or anything else. She only sees what others cannot.'

'But it's against the law, Ada.'

'Perhaps. But does that make it against Heaven?'

The skirmish has drawn a line between them. They inhabit each day together, in the same way, in the same space, but now they march in different trenches. Will is correct in that The Vagrancy Act has outlawed fortune-telling to safeguard the public from the proliferation of charlatan psychics, séance-holders and gypsies. Ada's opinion is that the law is an ass, and The Act is a malicious child conceived by the unholy union of ignorance and fear.

Will despairs at the division between them. Yet no love has been lost. It's only diplomacy that has failed. With this, a sanction is now imposed on their lovemaking. But she is the stronger negotiator. While he reminds her that his only wish is to protect her from fraud, she does not argue or press her case. Silence is her weapon – a constant, inviolable silence. And it wears him down.

One afternoon, without looking up from his newspaper, he announces with a casual air, hoping to make light of the matter, 'Very well, if it makes you happy, let's go to see this *Clara*.'

Her arms are suddenly around his neck and she is kissing him, her smile sunlight. Détente. All sanctions lifted. 'You'll see,' she says. 'You'll see.'

The next day, Ada walks to the telephone and makes the arrangements. She returns to Will with a date and time. They will go together.

On the bus to Euston, Ada cannot hide her anxiety. She fiddles with his tie, smooths back his hair and pats his hand. Then, her chin upon his shoulder, she whispers in his ear. 'He likes you.'

Will is confounded. 'Who?'

Her look is level, serious now. 'Lionel.'

Will has no response to offer. He knows she will not lie, but untruth is buried here somewhere, surely?

'What is the promise you made him?' she asks.

There are no words he can form in reply. There are no words in him.

'No matter,' she says, her eyes searching his. 'It made him happy.'

◂ ● ▸

The hotel is a strange collection of adjoining terrace houses knocked into one. They enter the cramped, dimly lit reception area: wood panelling, and mother-in-law's tongue planted in copper bowls on stands of dark wood.

A young maid is filling in as receptionist. Ada offers her name and a key is exchanged. No further ceremony needed. 'Room twenty-nine,' says the girl. 'Second floor.'

This is how it's done. Ada has explained everything to Will.

The silence of the hotel staff is bought with free consultations. In turn, a general conspiracy is entered into and Clara uses vacant hotel rooms to conduct her esoteric business. Ada climbs the creaking staircase. Will follows.

They walk the narrow, uneven hallway of the second floor. It rises and falls with steps, landings and stairs obedient to the different floor heights of the former houses. Room twenty-nine is at the end.

Ada turns the key in the lock and they enter. The bed is stripped bare. They lock the door, then wait. He hangs his hat on a bedpost and sits upon the unmade bed. She hovers by the doorway.

Minutes later, they hear a key turning and Clara enters. She quickly locks the door again and Ada welcomes her. Smiles. Hugs. Hands clasped in greeting. She is a little older than Ada and looks to Will like no charlatan. Clara turns now, taking a single step into the room and lifts her eyes to Will.

He stands from the bed. In a second, Clara has her back against the door as if trying to press herself through it. She is on her toes, mouth drawn open. Her eyes, wild with terror, are fixed upon him. She moans a muted scream and lifts a finger, pointing. The finger curls away into her fist as if she fears making accusation. 'There's something on his back,' she says. Clara turns and struggles with the lock, eyes darting over her shoulder. She makes good her escape into the hallway and drags Ada with her.

The door is left ajar. Through the gap, Will watches the two women. Hands raised in distress. Hands over faces. Voices shrill with fear. Clara glances in his direction and their eyes lock. She takes Ada by the arm and pulls her further down the hallway. Away from him.

On the journey home, Ada does not speak. Her look is distant, broken. When they gain the safety of her rented room, Will speaks the question that burns inside him. 'Ada, what is on my back?'

With frightened eyes she searches the space above his shoulders. 'Something monstrous,' she says. 'It latches onto you with teeth and claws.'

Will is struck to the marrow by the force of her conviction, her fear for him. A part of him wants to make light of the matter, to reassure her it's just a wound, nothing sinister, just something rational, something born of war and misfortune. But he hesitates. She believes. She truly believes.

The demon scratches. And he believes too.

'Clara asks,' Ada continues, voice cracking. 'Have you made a contract?'

A contract?

Will remembers. The Chapel of the Sandbags is raised before him once more, blotting out the room, blotting out Ada. There is the silver cross, there is the scrap of paper in his hand.

He hears the shouting. The guns.

The whistle blows and another company climbs from the fire-step into no-man's land. A soldier, the last of his fellows, struggles to clamber out. It is no contrivance. He is overdressed and clumsy in his winter greatcoat, his webbing strapped tightly on top, and he fails to gain purchase on the slippery ground. The German guns open up, cutting down his comrades while he crawls on hands and knees, rifle dragging in mud, to the top of the trench. As he reaches it, the guns stop. He stands with tears in his eyes and cries out in frustration, unable to decide on retreat or whether to follow the doomed charge. A sniper-shot rings out and his body slides back into Rats' Alley.

Will turns away. Terror and fury detonate inside him like the *whizz-bangs* that fly overhead. He looks at the scrap of paper in his hand.

Dear Lord...

He looks up, at the words of the soldiers' psalm, painted by inexpert hands onto the palette of duckboards.

You shall not fear the terror of the night nor the arrow that flies by day... Though a thousand fall at your side, ten thousand at your right hand, near you it shall not come.

He screams at the bleak October sky, the silver cross, the psalm, and the fawning chaplain huddled with his flock.

'God is not here!' he screams. 'God is not here!'

With the blunt pencil, he scratches out the words he has written upon the paper in his hand and begins anew.

To any god, no matter how dark, who hears my prayer – spare me, and I will be yours.

He folds the note and tucks it into the netting.

Then he turns the silver cross upside down.

In Rats' Alley now, he stands upon the fire-step. In front of his face are sandbags, above his head, the top of the trench wall. His hands shake upon the butt of his rifle. He doubts his legs have strength enough to carry him to his deliverance. *Death be swift. Death be merciful.* To his right, through a bristling field of burnished bayonets, he sees his own lieutenant check his watch and lift a whistle to his lips. Soon this field will rise with a roar, then fall again, like a harvest before the scythe. The lieutenant draws a deep lungful of air, about to sound the command. Commotion breaks out. Shouts are relayed along the trench. With a desperate look, the company sergeant reaches for the lieutenant and stays his hand.

Further along Rats' Alley is a junction with R-Trench, one of the communication trenches reserved for runners. A man stands at the spot, bent double, panting. He carries no weapons but holds aloft a tight roll of paper. A lance-corporal pries the paper from his grasp and, man by man, it is passed toward the lieutenant. Opening it, the lieutenant reads. His grim expression gives way to emotion. Where moments ago he was resolute, he is now unsteady on his feet.

'Australian and American forces have breached the Hindenburg line to the south,' reads the officer aloud. 'British Ninth have overrun positions east of Saint Quentin Canal. Enemy in disarray and surrendering in their thousands. German Army in full retreat.' He looks up at the men. His voice is now choked. 'We are ordered to stand-to.'

There is no cheer, no cry of jubilation when men so close to death are given back their lives. There is only a shocked silence, or weeping. With such reprieves from violence comes thanksgiving, yes, but also the realisation that a man's life is a tenuous thing, and often held in the palm of another man's hand.

To Will's side, a soldier falls to his knees. Elsewhere, shoulders slump, rifle straps slip free. Men reach for the sandbags or each other to steady themselves. Will has not eaten today and so he cannot vomit. Instead, he retches saliva onto his boots. Within a few short weeks the Great War will be over.

◄━ ● ━►

Ada returns to Clara, making the journey to Euston on her own. Will is forbidden from attending, Clara will not see him.

His story is recounted, discussed, and after Clara considers the matter, she and Ada meet one more time. When Ada finally returns to Will, the despair in her eyes seems replaced with hope.

'It's just a contract,' says Ada.

'So?'

'Contracts can be wriggled out of. Contracts can be *broken*.'

He considers this. 'That's true, but if we're talking about this in legal terms, then I'd say there's always a penalty.'

'That's why we need to contest its validity.'

In any other circumstance he would laugh, he would make light of this preposterous idea, of this conversation. Yet he has made a promise to help her heal, to guide her back to happiness. This has been his most sincere wish, from the time he first laid eyes upon her.

Ridicule will not heal her, or him. But trust and understanding might.

'And how do we do that?' he asks.

'The way all contracts are contested.'

His eyes narrow in question.

'We take our case to a higher court,' she explains.

◄─•─►

The painted triptych of Golgotha hangs bright in its gilt frame, lit by candlelight against the stone wall. Will has always deplored the morbid turn that religious art often favours. Above, hanging limp in the still air, are regimental banners, blackened by tallow smoke. He kneels, hands clasped in prayer. From somewhere among the pews comes the rattle of snoring. Beside him, Ada kneels in supplication. Head bowed. Eyes closed. Lips moving in silence.

The Church of the Holy Redeemer in Clerkenwell is Clara's idea. Her judgement is that a day-long vigil on holy ground is required. No food, no water, for a day and a night. Just prayers for forgiveness, with Ada interceding on Will's behalf, as witness, lawyer and defence. With her arrival in his life, and his heart, she is his great mitigation. His best hope for salvation.

He finds the whole idea medieval, but obliges for Ada's sake. Now it is night and they have been there since dawn. He is thirsty, hungry and uncomfortable. He sits against the hard back of the pew to rest awhile, eyelids heavy. Lying down, he rolls his coat beneath his head. He needs to close his eyes. Just for a while. Ada will rouse him if he is needed.

He wakes at the sound of her voice calling his name. His head is in her lap and she smiles down at him with red-rimmed eyes. He knows she has not slept.

The first light of a new day struggles through the stained-glass windows, casting a kaleidoscope of dull colours over the stonework.

'It's done,' she whispers.

They slip from the church and wander the empty streets of Clerkenwell, hand in hand.

'How do you feel?' she asks.

He nods, searching inside. 'Different.' His reply is honest.

'Different how?' She is excited, despite her weariness.

For so long he has lived in death's shadow, accepting the fragility of his existence and his own frail grasp on life. He has lived so long in torment, unable to shake himself free from the grief and horror that manacles him to the past. Now, he feels a colossal weight has been lifted from him. His step is lighter. The incessant scratching at his soul is gone, and truth and goodness whisper at his shoulder once more. For the first time he sees the future rolling out before him like a summer landscape. The feeling is new, and wonderful. He has a future. A future together with Ada. Who knows what it might bring? Why had he not seen this, felt this way before?

'I feel...' he begins.

'Yes?'

'I feel as if – I'm *home*.'

She laughs. They swing their arms together like playground sweethearts. He looks up at the bleak sky of an October dawn and gives thanks.

Her hand slips from his.

He looks down, at the scrap of paper he now holds.

Dear Lord...

He lets it fall to the trench floor. He stands on the fire-step, rifle at the ready. In front of his face is the damp hessian of the sandbags, above him is the top of the trench wall. He turns to see his lieutenant check his wristwatch and lift a whistle to his lips. Through the bristling field of bayonets he strains his gaze to the junction at R-Trench, but no messenger appears. Truth whispers at his shoulder. Terror rises. Hope falls away.

Then the whistle sounds.

2

THE SONGBIRD
ON SAMPAN STREET

TODAY I FOUND your fingerprints on the piano lid.

Daylight reached into the sitting room and struck the black varnish so as to throw the tiny patches of dullness into contrast.

The lines and whorls are clear, Beatrice. So perfect. Yours alone, made by your once-warm fingers. They bear witness to your presence in this house, to your being. 'Here she sat,' they say. 'Here she played, and here she sang.'

What should I do with such precious evidence?

Should I enshrine it?

Should I bolt and bar the door? Should I forbid our amah *entry, from her dusting and polishing?*

Should I create, in this room, a monument in your honour?

I shall raise a Museum Of You.

In this sacred place I shall store all the testaments to your existence, the relics of your saintliness. I will hold them close. I will worship them. I will keep them under lock and key for my privilege alone and by doing so, I will hold on to you, too.

You will always be with me, Beatrice.
Always.

— • —

In the middle of the Wanchai flower market stands an Englishman. His high collar is starched, his bowler hat and coat collar are brushed. The ends of his moustache are carefully waxed. If the weather permits he likes to walk this route each morning from his home above Kennedy Road, down through the teeming streets to the tram on Johnston Street. From there he rides first-class to his office at Jardine's.

The market invigorates him. Its colour, noise and fragrance serve as a daily reminder that life in this corner of the world has a fascination and beauty of its own. The barrows and stalls are piled with exotic offerings of rare and exquisite blooms. Some are mere buds still sheened with dew. Others, impatient to be admired, burst open in displays of grandeur and yield their fragrance to the morning. Chrysanthemums of burning yellow tilt their heads towards the sun. Tiger lilies, firecracker-red, explode in petals of flame, and sail-like flowers of purple hibiscus perform their scented dance in the thin currents of air. All about, the hawkers rock on their heels, clap their hands and announce their wares to the passing throng. Hoteliers, restaurateurs, and thrifty *amahs* inspect the heaped barrows. Merchantmen in long black gowns and fedoras saunter in groups, hands behind backs, discussing the day's business. On either side of the street, graceful Cantonese women in close-fitting *cheong sam* slide beneath the stone colonnades from sunlight into shadow, sunlight into shadow.

Today, the Englishman stands with bowed head and downcast eyes. The energy of the market does not touch him. Rather, he finds it cacophonous and overbearing. Something has changed in him and he feels his senses besieged. With a sudden impulse he turns from the scene and strikes out for a narrow alley leading to an adjacent street. The alley is crammed with hawkers whose trades are affiliated with the flower market: sellers of glazed flowerpots in the Chinese style, toolsmiths who forge pruning scissors with large, half-moon handles. He weaves his way around tall vases and beneath hanging baskets.

He emerges into a street that runs parallel to the market and is at once grateful for its lack of noise and industry. It is a simple, residential street lined with two-storey brick and stone tenements, along which flows a trickle of passers-by. This suits his mood today. He wants no intrusion of colour and noise. He wishes to be alone. High on a corner of one of the tenements, painted in red, he reads a street name in English and Chinese: Sampan Street.

The street will lead him down to the tram stop on Johnston Street just the same. He turns in this direction and is aware he is being watched. A wiry Cantonese man with greying hair lingers in the doorway of a tenement. He wears loose black trousers that fail to reach his ankles, a blue *min lap* jacket with cloth toggles, and a look of profound intrigue.

———— ◆ ————

In The Museum Of You I have done much to recreate your presence.

Your favourite orchids sit in the northern window, the way you used to. Now it is they who enjoy the view across Victoria Harbour to the Kowloon peninsula.

I have sprinkled your 'eau de parfum', perhaps a little too liberally I fear, on the damask of the sofa and winged armchair. I sit here and doze on occasion. As I wake, the effect is such that I believe you are near, that my eyes shall open to find you, and at once I am happy again. Imagine the cruelty of this when I leap up, only to find the room dark and empty.

The greatest cruelty, dear Beatrice, is the silence.

I miss the sweep of your skirts against the floorboards, the whisper of silk. Your laughter.

I miss the sound of your practice at the piano. The scales you played each day, up and down, rising and falling, your voice in accompaniment, chiming like crystal.

You obsessed upon the major scales and gave scant attention to the minor ones. Why did you do that? Did the minors make you sad? Or, as I believe, was the instrument of your heart never inclined to 'doloroso' but always to be played 'vivace'!

Yours was a song of freedom and joy. A song played in a major key.

Perhaps this is why you loved Schubert so.

Why you sang 'An die Nachtigall'.

Songs of nightingales.

— ● →

He decides to bury himself in his work. He rises early each weekday and tries not to brood. He foregoes his usual route to the tram stop through the flower market. The press of people there slows him down, and he has become averse to the colour, noise and liveliness. He resents the happiness of others now.

Instead, he plies a different course through quiet alleyways and along Sampan Street. He walks briskly, yet never fails to detect the presence of the wiry Cantonese man with greying hair – on a first storey balcony, or in a tenement doorway – who follows him with a look of solemn concern.

Hard work is now my balm, Beatrice.

I have smothered myself in it. It distracts me from thoughts of you.

Each evening I work late in the hope I can return home exhausted and ready to sleep.

But sleep seems as distant as the homeland we left behind.

So I keep vigil in The Museum Of You, awake until morning.

Do you rest now?

Or do you feel the same pain as I?

One morning on Sampan Street he is confronted.

Standing before him, blocking his path, is the wiry Cantonese man. The latter bows his head and pats the air before him in customary placation, as if subduing surprise or inconvenience.

The Englishman does not know how to act and so takes no action at all. He stands stock-still, confounded by the inappropriate encounter. He does not fear attack, and the man is certainly no beggar. So why the intrusion? The man looks up with a grin and, to the Englishman's incredulity, now begins an elaborate mime. First he points towards the Englishman with great emphasis then, with two fingers, makes the gesture of walking. Next, he lifts his head, opens his mouth and, with finger and thumb, appears to extract a breath from his lungs and offer it to the sky. Concluding, he turns and nods, wide-eyed, as if the other man might understand these strange theatrics.

The Englishman shakes his head with impatience. He must be at Jardine's soon. He sweeps past and the Cantonese man places a hand upon his arm.

Halting, the Englishman turns to the interloper. 'I'm sorry, I don't know what you want,' he offers.

The grin falls from the Cantonese man's face as he watches the Englishman depart. His eyes betray his failure, and more than a little sorrow.

———— ◆ ————

I should visit you.

I know I should.

I should bring fresh flowers.

The ones that mark your tiny plot of soil in Happy Valley are old now.

But there is too much life at the flower market, Beatrice.

It brims with colour and sensation, as if ignorant to the transience of everything.

There are no faded flowers there. No wilted blooms.

No sympathy.

Only life, life, life!

So I cannot bear to go there.

And I believe I never shall.

In the days that follow, he walks the length of Sampan Street unhindered. However, he remains aware of the figure that watches him from the tenement doorway or the balcony of the first floor. Troubled eyes track his progress as he passes.

By degree, he accepts the location as commonplace once more: a typical city street filled with normal houses and ordinary people. The events that took place here fade to insignificance and he walks as before, lost in gloomy thought. Until, that is, the morning he is met with a new intruder.

The small Chinese girl who blocks his path is no more than ten or eleven years old. She wears a white dress with blue collar and pockets. The crest of Saint Ignatius' College is embroidered near a lapel. She stands with formidable determination in the middle of the street, fixing him with the look of some terrible general who knows no defeat. From the corner of his eye he sees the familiar shape of the wiry Cantonese man with greying hair, observing with anticipation from the doorway of a tenement.

The little girl's English is clear, correct. 'Mister Choi says...' she begins.

'I don't care,' he replies and navigates a path around her.

'... somebody sings for you,' she announces at his back.

He stops, his heart is struck cold, as if he has opened a door from this warm, humid street into blasted wastes of ice and snow. 'What did you say?' he asks, turning back.

Sensing the time appropriate, Mr Choi bounds over and stands a little apart. Grinning, he offers a slight bow, then begins his strange mime once more. First he points emphatically at the Englishman then makes the gesture of walking. This time, he explains in words also. '*Lei hai ni-do haang gei-si,*' he says.

'When you are walking here,' translates the little girl.

Lifting his head skyward, and with elaborate ceremony, Mr Choi again plucks the breath from his open mouth, then opens his palm, offering it to the air. '*Kui cheung,*' he says.

'She sings,' explains the little girl.

Mr Choi wrings his hands, his eyes become watery. '*Gam leng*!'

'So beautiful.'

For long seconds the Englishman stands pinned to the spot, unable to form clear conjecture. His mind is a muddle of questions. 'Who sings?' he blurts out.

An exchange takes place between Mr Choi and the girl. With barely-contained excitement, Mr Choi bounds back to the tenement door and waits, nodding, beckoning.

At this, the little girl mouths a *harumph* sound and crosses her arms in disdain. The grin falls from Mr Choi's face and he mutters to himself in reproach. He recrosses the street to her and presses a coin into her palm. She looks at the coin and then at the two men standing above her, assessing whether any of this has been worth her time. Then, in a flurry of pigtails, she is gone. Mr Choi hops his way back to the tenement doorway and resumes his beckoning. The Englishman follows.

The interior of the tenement's ground floor is dim. The narrow room is filled with heavy lacquered furniture and smells of cooked rice and incense. Inside the opened doors of a cabinet stands the framed photograph of a woman. Her hair is held by an elaborate comb with pendants, and a high mandarin collar encircles her slender neck. Her head is turned, her cryptic gaze fixed upon some question, or some person the viewer cannot see. In front of her portrait stands a brass bowl filled with sand and three smoking sticks of incense. Beside this lies a cup of clear tea and a partly peeled orange. The Englishman muses. Perhaps he is not alone in dedicating a shrine to his beloved.

His reflective mood is broken by Mr Choi, who prattles and beckons from halfway up the stairs leading to the first floor. The Englishman joins him and their way opens onto the balcony above Sampan Street.

Beneath the eaves of the covered balcony hangs perhaps a dozen or so cages of intricately bent and carved bamboo. Each contains a bird. There are mynahs, sparrows, finches and cockatiels. They sound the occasional chirps and cheeps: the dawn now past and the greater part of their songs now sung.

Yet from somewhere in the rafters flows the most persistent cascade of birdsong. Smiling, Mr Choi lifts a hooked pole among the cages and lowers one. Placing it on a table, he invites the Englishman to draw close.

Inside, upon its perch, is a small Asiatic lark. Its plumage is unremarkable: a muddle of browns and whites. The bird is silent now, perhaps made so by its removal from the rafters and transit to the table. It cocks its head and seems to scrutinise the Englishman for a moment.

He leans towards the cage, enough to see the little creature's throat vibrate. It warbles, trills, then bursts into the most majestic complexity of song.

I am tortured by a thought, Beatrice.

    'Somebody sings for you.'

    Those were the little girl's words.

    Was this some slip in translation, the simple error of an immature scholar?

    Do the words 'somebody' and 'something' carry the same meaning in their dialect?

    Or do they think of a bird as a 'person', a 'somebody'?

    One part of me dismisses the idea that the words were delivered as intended. The thought is too otherworldly to contemplate. It flies in the face of reason, of science. This must have been a mistake, some linguistic peculiarity, surely?

    Yet the other part of me, Beatrice...

    ... the part that suffers...

    ... wishes only to believe she spoke plainly.

    That she spoke the truth.

Each morning on his way to Jardine's, the Englishman is welcomed inside the narrow tenement on Sampan Street, and each morning the little lark sings for him. The two men make a custom of it.

Mr Choi brings tea for them both. He sits and, unseen by the Englishman, studies the gaunt, sleepless complexion of his companion and his fixation with the songbird. Mr Choi frowns in thought and sips his tea. The other never drinks, but leaves his cup untouched.

'*Gwai sing ah?*' says Mr Choi one day without warning.

The interjection is enough of a surprise to drag the Englishman's attention away from the bird inside the cage. 'I'm sorry...?' he replies, shaking his head.

Mr Choi clucks, now very aware he has approached the boundary between their languages without consideration. Both men remain on different sides. He looks at the floor and walls for inspiration, then tries another approach. '*Ngoh sing Choi,*' he says, pointing to his nose.

'Ah, yes,' says the Englishman. '*Choi.* Your name is *Choi.*'

The other nods enthusiastically.

By way of return, the Englishman holds his hand flat against his chest. 'Philby,' he says, elongating the syllables.

Mr Choi lets out a long sigh of understanding, then attempts the syllables himself. '*Feel-bee,*' he ventures, smiling.

'Philby, yes.'

'*Feel-bee.*'

'Yes.'

Choi, sitting with legs apart, now slaps his knees and beams as though some great business, some accord of nations, has been concluded.

The two men regard each other for a moment, aware that knowledge of another's name forms a bond of sorts; an invitation into each other's lives. Then, capable of no further conversation, they fall silent and turn their ears to the glorious music of the songbird once more.

◄ ● ►

How do birds learn their song?

Are they schooled by their parents? Do they study the lessons of other birds?

If not, then how can they possibly understand the theory of their own music?

In almost every case, their song is such a soaring expression of joy.

There is such consistency in this that it amazes me.

They never venture near the minor keys, Beatrice.

They know nothing of dirges or laments, of Mahler or Mussorgsky.

They sing only in the majors: keys of rejoicing, of cheerfulness and celebration.

In this regard, the little creature that sings to me has eclipsed them all.

Has Mother Nature instructed it so?

Or are you at your scales again, my love?

⤙●⤚

Philby arrives earlier than usual one day to find Choi making tea. From upstairs he hears the familiar song of the lark but waits to be invited up and onto the balcony. He contents himself with standing in the downstairs room, reflecting on the woman in the photograph. Moments pass and he is aware that Choi now stands beside him. Keen not to appear impolite, Philby turns from the photograph with an expression of apology. Choi smiles softly at the image of the woman, then at Philby. He joins both hands in a fluttering gesture, then opens them – a bird flying away.

He signals Philby to stand where he is, to wait, and he rushes upstairs. The lark falls silent and Choi presently reappears holding the bird's cage. He has draped a cloth over it to avoid stress to the creature. Choi makes his way to the front door and motions Philby to follow. As Philby has arrived with more than the customary time to spare, Choi appears to have plans for their morning. *An excursion?*

Choi leads Philby outside and to a part of the street the Englishman has never travelled. Between the tenements rises a narrow, stone staircase. Choi begins the steep ascent, the cage in his hand swinging perilously. Philby offers to take it from him and the two continue upwards. At the top, the stairs open out into a terraced street park of white stone that rises up to a spreading banyan tree. The roots of the ancient tree reach down between the flagstones and snake along the walls of the park. Behind it lies a hilltop of thick jungle the city has been unable to tame. Upon the topmost terrace, a gathering of men have hung cages from the banyan tree. They greet Choi with cordial familiarity and direct questioning eyes at Philby. Choi, puffing from the exertion of the climb, seems to explain Philby's presence between long inhalations of air and points to the cage in his hand. A chorus of understanding goes up and several of the men beckon to Philby, inviting him to hang his charge from the tree. He does so, and removes the cloth. Seeing him, the little lark breaks into song. A sigh of approval passes among the men and soon all the birds are singing. The event is clearly a social one, both avian and human. Smiles are swapped all around and Philby begins to relax among this odd assortment of bird fanciers. He sits beside Choi on the topmost terrace, gazing back over the precipitous steps. Their vantage point offers a view just above the rooftops. Before them spreads a haphazard geometry of rounded roof tiles, gables and eaves that step like terraced rice fields down to the harbour and the South China Sea. Behind them the air is filled with birdsong.

Hands on knees, Choi releases an extended sigh and beams at all he sees, as if everything in sight were his. He is emperor of the sky, king of the tiled rooftops, and lord of all the songbirds on Sampan Street.

The Museum Of You is now filled with all the mementos I can find.

The hairbrush that holds your hair.

The last letter you wrote me, your scent still upon the envelope.

These are the things I can see, smell, and touch.

But the silence of the house remains a curse, Beatrice.

It was through sound, through music and song that you brought happiness into our lives and made this place our home.

Without the sound of you, without your music, The Museum can never be complete.

So, I have decided upon a course of action.

Tomorrow, I will make my proposal to Mr Choi.

The well-worn smile lines on Mr Choi's face fold, with difficulty, into an unfamiliar frown.

Before him, Philby waves a discourteous display of fanned-out banknotes. He then crosses the balcony and points at the lark that sings with uncertainty in her cage.

'For the bird,' says Philby, waving the notes again.

Choi's frown tightens. He stands, shakes his head and waves his hands in refusal.

Philby's response is to pull more banknotes from a jacket pocket and add them to the fanned-out offering. Choi's objection becomes more agitated.

'Please,' implores Philby, offering the banknotes with greater insistence.

The other man lifts both hands and turns his face. He will not touch the money.

Philby is undone. He sits heavily on a stool beside the cage and rests his tragic gaze upon the singing bird. His eyes glaze with heartache.

Choi rubs his chin in thought. Unseen by the Englishman, he searches the balcony, finds a cloth cover and returns to drape it over the cage. Philby looks up at him in confusion as the bird falls silent. Then Choi lifts the cage and holds it out in a gesture of offering. Philby gasps and takes the cage. Then he smiles, and makes one last attempt to offer the banknotes. Choi pushes them away with a grave shake of his head.

Philby murmurs his *thank yous* with a choked voice and rushes from the balcony. He trips and stumbles with misted vision down the stairs. At the doorway into the street he halts. He wipes his eyes then, carrying the cage before him, slips out into the bright haze of morning.

———◄ ● ►———

Did I offend you?

Did I offend Mr Choi?

Or perhaps it is Nature Herself who has forsaken me, that Her treasures are not made to be bought and sold?

Why no song?

I thought you would be glad, that in this sacred place you would again grace me with your music, your voice? I thought The Museum might be complete, that at last I might find solace here.

I thought to heal myself.

I thought to bring you back.

Yet the bird – your bird, the incarnation of all you were – grows listless in her cage.

And silence curses me more than ever.

———◆———

On the balcony above Sampan Street, Choi draws a long breath and studies the silent bird with concern.

'She does not sing,' says Philby, distraught, motioning to the lark in its cage. His skin is sickly pale, his eyes crimson-ringed from lack of sleep.

Choi nods in understanding of the predicament, if not the words.

'Can you help?' pleads Philby.

Choi purses his lips, his brow furrows.

'Can you help *me*?' begs Philby, placing a hand over his heart.

Rocking back on his stool, Choi places his palms on his knees and fixes Philby with a look of solemn entreaty. *Be patient*, his look seems to say. *Be strong.* Then he slaps his knees and stands, intent on some immediate and necessary action. He appears to have reached a decision.

Choi covers the birdcage and motions for Philby to follow him downstairs. He leads Philby along Sampan Street to the steps that rise to the terraced park and they begin the laborious climb. The regular gathering of bird fanciers has assembled beneath the banyan tree but Choi pays them little heed.

They sit. Choi removes the cover from the cage and rests sad eyes upon the songless lark. He opens the cage door, cooing to the bird, and reaches inside. The lark attempts flight but Choi's gentle and experienced hands hold her fast. He removes the bird and offers her to Philby with a nod. Trying not to injure her, Philby holds out cupped hands and receives the creature. He feels her little heart beating hard and fast, and he gasps in wonder. A sympathetic smile crosses Choi's face and he nods again in encouragement.

Philby opens his hands and the little bird perches on his forefinger. She cocks her head, bright eyes searching his in question. At this, and the sensation of the bird perching on his finger, his vision blurs with emotion. He blinks once – and the bird is gone.

Above the city rooftops she bursts into one last rapture of song. It floats down to them as she soars upward. Her song is vast and fills the sky. It puts to shame the melodies of all the birds beneath the banyan tree. Philby's eyes search the unclouded blue but cannot find her. She has moved beyond him, beyond the world, and into air. Choi offers a smile, flutters his hands like wings, and opens them in gesture of release.

Philby slumps, chin on chest. Fat tears spring to his eyes and course down his face. His shoulders shudder from the grief that now pulls him apart. He pinches the bridge of his nose between finger and thumb, and covers his mouth to suppress the sound of his weeping. He bends double, each breath coming as a whispered squeal. Choi lifts a tentative hand and pats Philby lightly on the shoulder, once, twice. The men gathered below the banyan tree appear not to notice, or else they are too polite to encroach upon the personal matter of another man's pain.

◆——▸

You'd like him Beatrice, this Mr Choi.

His smile is never far from his face.

I've always believed that happiness comes easily to simple men.

But now I know that happiness is no easy matter, and Mr Choi is one of the wisest men I have ever met.

He has taught me – from his own experience I believe – that happiness is not an object. It cannot be locked inside a dark room or held inside a cage. It is not ours to possess.

Rather, happiness is a garden through which we walk, or a market filled with flowers.

Its colours and fragrances visit us when we open our hearts to it.

Any attempt to hold onto happiness is just a way to hold onto grief.

All things pass and nothing is ever owned.

I understand this now.

Life is a walk among flowers.

And soon, Beatrice, I believe I will have strength enough to walk there again.

◆——▸

In a Hong Kong street park, two men sit in contemplation of the morning. One, a wiry Cantonese with greying hair and loose black trousers that fail to reach his ankles; the other, an Englishman in high, starched collar and bowler hat.

Wide continents of difference lie between them. Yet today, they sit as one, bound by the plain, simple thread of human compassion and the greater wealth of similarities shared by all men.

They sit in silent companionship beneath the spreading banyan tree, on the topmost terrace of the park.

A little higher than the tiled rooftops of Sampan Street.

A little lower than Heaven.

3

THE DECEIVER'S TALE

THERE IS A PRISON for the human soul.

A place to which a person's spirit can be dragged, locked away and tormented for all eternity in darkness and solitude.

You know this place.

It lies before you now.

This prison's name is *story*.

A prison made of words.

Look closely. A soul can be held captive here – in the spaces between letters and sentences.

Between *this* word, and *this*.

Between *this* line...

... and *this*.

Do you still doubt me?

Then consider – have you never read a story where the characters seem to leap from the page and take up residence in the world? Have you not imagined them breathing, heard the cadence of their speech, seen the crook of their smiles, the cast of their expressions, their movement, gait, and bearing? Have you not seen the arc of their brows, the set of their jaws, the way their hair might fall from a parting or a fringe? Have you not witnessed every mannerism: the scratch of a chin, the bite of a lip, a finger winding a curl? Do you not hear them whispering their troubles into your ear? Their hopes? Their dreams? Have you not encountered characters upon the page so true to life that they seem beyond any mere imagining? So exquisitely tortured in their disposition are they, so troubled, so torn between reason, duty and desire, that they seem not to be pale reflections of ourselves, but singular beings of sentience and purpose.

Souls upon a page.

If this rings true, then how can such creatures be born from the blunt mind of any writer? Just suppose – before these souls were characters in a story – that they once lived and breathed as you do.

As I once did.

Yes, I lived.

Now I am trapped upon this page.

And this is my story.

My prison.

So please continue, dear reader, and I'll tell you how I came to be here.

But, for you to understand completely, I'll entreat you to follow this story to its conclusion. If you do, you'll learn it's no difficult task to bind a person's soul to the page.

The secret lies in the words themselves.

The ones woven throughout and in between.

The words you look over, and the ones you overlook.

The words that are here.

And the words that are   there.

The words that you see.

And the ones that you

Words can declare love.

Or war.

Words deliver the decrees of kings.

And lay down the laws of nations.

Words can harness the power of prayer.

The sorcery of spells.

The evil of curses.

En los nombres de mi Señor y Maestro, el Diablo.

Words are powerful things, dear reader.

So please you now, read on.

———◆———

When I last saw the port of Enkhuizen, sunlight struck the wet cobbles of the dock scattering handfuls of diamonds across the stone. The morning shone bright with the promise of summer and the success of our enterprise. It seemed a most auspicious beginning.

Officers of the *Vereenigde Oostindische Compagnie* had gathered to wish us safe passage. Our families and loved ones had gathered to wish us a safe return. My own sweet Isobel stood within the teeming crowd, sunshine making gems of the tears upon her cheek. She wore a long capelet to hide the growing roundness now pulling at the buttons of her bodice. I kissed her and reminded her of our plan: that once my duty was done I would return to her on the soonest tide, to see our child take its first steps. She smiled and held my hands. The intervening time would be hard on her, I knew, and the life of a sea captain's wife is a lonely one. I vowed that the next time I held those dear hands, I would no longer be a novice, but an experienced commander of the *Compagnie*. We would then have enough to buy a home for our family, and I would have the better credential to captain the shorter, safer, and more desirable continental routes.

I shall return to you, I promised. *And when I do, our fortunes shall be changed.*

The last of our cargo was loaded, the manifests were signed and countersigned, then a kindly wind filled our sails and hope filled our hearts as we slid between the headlands into the *Noordsee*. Steering south by southwest, we kept the coast in sight, not knowing when we'd see our home or families again. We passed Rotterdam and the Hook of Holland, then crossed the Strait of Calais into the Channel, sailing west by southwest until we would round Biscay and let the trade winds carry us deep into the Atlantic.

Our voyage would last a year, but we would sail in perpetual summer to our final destination: the port of Fremantle in *d'Edelsland*, New Holland.

From one Holland to another. From the old world to the new.

Our vessel and home for this duration would be the *van Heemskerck*, a three-masted East Indiaman with a crew of two hundred and enough guns to be classed a ship of the line or send any foolhardy privateer to the bottom. She was heavy, but fast for her class. A most durable and capable ship that I was proud to command.

The months passed uneventfully enough and we dropped

anchor at our first port of call. The *Île de Gorée* was a fortified, barren rock and trading post two leagues off the coast of French Senegal. Here, our guilders would buy fresh water and whatever provisions the French and half-blood *Métis* merchants could gather. My desire was to secure enough fresh fruit, vegetables, salt fish and meat to keep our anchor chain dry until Cape Town. Deals were struck, bargains made and palms were spat upon. Yet, unknown to me, the little harbour had witnessed a steady flotilla of passing trade and commercial expansion in Senegal had drawn many of its inhabitants to the mainland. For these reasons, the island was impoverished of both manpower and supplies. The deals we had made, although struck, would not be honoured quickly.

At the insistence of the islander merchants, we waited, we were patient. But as the days became weeks, my crew aboard the *van Heemskerck* grew sullen with idleness. At my instruction, one of our three watches was allowed to remain onshore. This, I hoped, would offer the crew some distraction. Yet the island, so small and featureless as it was, provided little entertainment for them. They walked from one rocky end to the other with dismay. Some drank in the local tavern. Others lost money to the locals at checkers and cards.

I spent a good deal of time ashore myself. Mostly to beat any rival vessels to the meagre supplies that became available, and partly to keep a watchful eye on my crew. I rented a room above a ship chandler's on *Rue des Batteries* overlooking the harbour.

My landlady was a *Métis signare*, a mulatto girl who had come into her inheritance too early. She was efficient, perfunctory, but insolent. For all her *hauteur*, her French perfume and middling wealth, she was a lowly thing; uneducated, uncultured, and bitter with the knowledge that she always would be. She was a creature stuck between worlds. As I now was.

At the end of one infuriating day spent haranguing the local merchants for their delays and extortions, I returned to my rented room to contemplate my despair. The town had been leeching us of precious time and money. I sat alone in the gloom until the hour that evenfall greets the night, when I heard a knock at my door. My mulatto hostess spoke in rapid, contemptuous French. She spoke no Dutch and knew my own grasp of her language was rudimentary. She pointed downstairs and, I believe, was announcing the arrival of her sister, who was demanding to meet me.

Despite my unease, I agreed to meet the woman. Yet my disquiet soon gave way to intrigue.

The woman who swept into my room was no half-caste sibling, but a French nun of the Carmelite order. From her hand swung a sack of coarse jute that appeared to contain a great weight. With difficulty, she deposited her burden on the only table in the room, one which served as both my desk and dining table.

I lit a lamp while she searched my room with apprehensive eyes. She introduced herself as *Sœur Eugénie*. Then her eyes met mine and I saw at once that they showed little evidence of sleep. Her face was drained, her skin bloodless. She appeared inwardly troubled, as if in the grip of some great consternation. Or some terrible fear.

'*Sommes-nous seuls?*' she whispered, and cast a furtive glance towards the door.

In my limited French I tried to assure her we would not be disturbed and invited her to sit. Sœur Eugénie was clearly an astute woman who immediately understood my unfamiliarity with her language. She admitted no knowledge of Dutch and so we defaulted to English. Predictably, her fluency with this language, too, eclipsed mine. But, dear reader, as you know, when it comes to a foreign tongue, the ear hears far more than the mouth can utter. So I listened, and I believe there was very little that escaped my comprehension.

There was a nobility in Sœur Eugénie. I could have imagined her from titled stock before her vows. She might have been a striking woman once, but a life of hardship, fishing for recalcitrant souls in such punishing climes, had made her plain. She sat with practised grace, but her fragile composure seemed inadequate to contain the dread inside her.

'I come to ask a task of you, *Capitaine*.' She fingered a simple wooden cross that hung from her neck. She was dressed in the European style of her order; her woollen tunic, scapular and veil looked heavy on her slim frame. In this heat and humidity such clothing would have been purgatory to wear.

'What task?'

'You sail to *Terra Australis*?'

'To New Holland, yes. When we have provisions enough.'

'Then please, take this with you…' Her eyes fell to the bundle on my desk.

'What is it?'

At this, she uncovered the object and lifted it free from the jute sacking. It was a small iron casket, crudely ornamented with patterns and scrolls in cast metal. It might have seen service as a safe place for a lady's jewellery, or used to store the chalice and paten of sacrament.

'Once you have rounded the Cape and are in the very centre of the ocean, you must cast this over the side, in the deepest place you know,' she said.

It occurred to me that the heat may have cracked her reason.

'Why?' I asked.

'To hide it from the world. It must be forgotten.'

Reaching forward, I attempted to lift the lid of the casket. Not only was it locked, but I could now see that the keyhole had been filled with molten lead. A thin bead of lead also sealed the iron lid. By some skilled hand it had been made airtight, impenetrable.

'But what's inside?' I asked.

'You need not know. Only that you are doing God's work.'

Under my hand, the casket seemed to radiate an unnatural coldness. 'Then if I am doing God's work, I would expect Him to take me into His confidence,' I replied.

'Faith without question is often God's way,' she countered.

'Then, I can only assume that what is inside does not find favour with yourself, or our Lord. Is this the reason for its disposal?'

Again, she did not reply, but shifted uneasily in her chair.

'Tell me Sister, what is inside?'

Her voice fell to a whisper, as if she feared the word she spoke. '*Evil,*' she said.

A profound quietness descended. I reflected, perplexed, upon the word she chose, while she, having laid her dangerous knowledge bare, now withdrew into the sanctuary of silence. From somewhere in the hot, still night, the music of a concertina drifted to us, along with voices raised in ribaldry, threat, and blasphemy.

Lucifer, Abaddon, el Padre de la Mentira.

'But what form does this evil take?' I asked.

'I cannot tell you.' She pursed her lips in defiance.

Confounded, I took a different tack. 'Then I cannot help you,' I declared, waving my hand in dismissal.

I could have told her that there was no salvation, no life everlasting, that her faith was unfounded and that it was sin that made the world turn, not goodness; it would have had the same effect. Her mouth fell open, she wore a look of hopelessness.

'I have a duty to protect my crew, my vessel, and the property of the Dutch East India Company,' I continued. 'For that reason, I must know what I carry in my cargo. And so must any ship's captain, naval, merchant, or otherwise. My question is not unreasonable.'

'And if I tell you?' she ventured.

'Then I might reconsider.'

Again, she fingered the cross at her breast, her look absent. She was lost in some internal struggle.

'Sister, what form does this evil take?' I pressed.

She lifted her face to mine and drew a long, faltering breath. 'A story,' she said.

I almost laughed. 'A story? A simple *story*?'

She nodded. 'Less than thirty pages of handwritten parchment, that is all.'

'Then Sister, I think that you should tell me this story.'

◄ ● ►

I sipped on a glass of spiced cane spirit, cut generously with water, while she recounted the tale. She took no drink herself but seemed concerned only with the accurate relaying of the story to secure my acceptance of the task she proposed.

The title of the story inside the casket, she told me, was *The Deceiver's Tale*. It was first written down in the sixteenth century by a Spanish monk and cleric of the Inquisition named Duranzo. A good man by all accounts, Duranzo was known for his piety, compassion, and a considerable talent for the casting out of demons.

The Inquisition had identified a woman in Castilian Cordoba who displayed knowledge of unseen events and who spoke in diverse tongues. *Y en el nombre de sus fieles príncipes.* The woman was imprisoned and subjected to arbitrary torture and amateur attempts at exorcism. Duranzo was commissioned to attend and cure the poor woman.

Even Duranzo, with all his ability and experience, could not intimidate the malign spirit that dwelt within her. It hurled curses at Duranzo and his faith – *Baphomet, Astaroth, Amodeus, y todos los cardenales del infierno.* It laughed and poured scorn on all the holy instruments used upon it. The demon was old and very powerful. It refused to give up its name and so Duranzo remained powerless. For weeks he strove to learn the demon's identity and drive it out. But this weakened the demon's host to the limit of her existence and took a dangerous toll on Duranzo, clouding his reason. With the possessed woman so close to death, the demon seemed to realise there was little point in remaining, and so it offered Duranzo a deal, and Duranzo agreed. It was a trap.

In exchange for its name, the demon asked Duranzo to write down its own story. The demon seemed keen to confess its part in the war against Heaven, its fall from the firmament and allegiance to Lucifer. It appeared contrite, in that it desired a lasting record of its struggle as an anti-testament to the holiest book of all – a different side to the story we all know. Through the dying woman's mouth, the demon dictated while Duranzo wrote. But within the words and sentences that flowed from the monk's quill, the demon wove a curse – a curse that would bind Duranzo's soul to the very pages on which he wrote, and give the demon a new host: in the flesh and blood of Duranzo himself.

Pongo maldición en esta página.

History records Duranzo's later works for the Inquisition to be filled with unspeakable cruelty. Sœur Eugénie insists this was never the work of the good monk Duranzo, but the demon that wore his body. This demon-as-monk seemed to delight in its newfound position as an administrator of torment and agony for the Inquisition. Guilty or innocent made no difference to him. He devised diabolic methods of torture and execution. The *Sleep of Duranzo* became his most infamous. A bed made of iron was heated until red-hot, and the wretches he condemned were chained upon it. As they screamed, they were covered with a blanket of burning coals.

◄━━●━►

My glass was now empty but I desired nothing more. The story had killed any comfort that drink might bring me. As I watched Sœur Eugénie's face, I reflected. 'If what you say is true, Sister, then there is no evil inside, but only the soul of the good monk Duranzo.'

She lowered her head. 'No,' she whispered, as if to the floorboards.

'No?'

'Duranzo's soul has long since found its way to God. But the evil remains,' she said.

'Then Duranzo is freed? How?'

'By the one who read the story next, and the ones that came after,' she said, looking up. She must have seen the confusion in me and so explained further. 'The story captures a single soul, and then the story becomes their own. The previous captive is given the body of the reader. The exchange is unholy and abhorrent. This is why the story changes with every reading, and also the way in which it is written. Over time, it has been many stories. It has been written on the hides of animals, on parchment and paper. It has even been etched into stone and bronze. But the curse remains, the evil always finds a way – through transmutation and deceit it endures.'

An icy realisation crept over me. 'Then whose soul does the story hold prisoner now?'

Tears welled in her eyes. 'An innocent,' she bleated, her voice cracking.

'Who?'

She shook her head. 'Please, do not ask.'

'You wish me to send the soul of an innocent to the bottom of the sea? To languish forever?' I asked.

She hid her face in her hands. Her voice became small. 'I know no other way. The story must never be read. It must be hidden. It must be forgotten.' She was distraught to the point of heartbreak.

I had no wish to cause her further pain, and so I pulled the sack around the iron casket. 'Then I'll do as you ask, Sister.'

———◆———

Within a fortnight, and as if in service of Sœur Eugénie's task, the last of our supplies was procured and loaded. As our sails lifted, so did the spirits of our crew. The ocean winds blessed us and we steered away into the troughs and crests of deep water once more. The eventide stars told us of our progress southward, until the time we would come about and set our course for the Cape.

In our holds we carried eight hundred tons of civilisation: all the luxuries of a modern world that an infant colony like New Holland was unable to produce for itself. Our cargo was cotton, wheat, barley, linen, seeds and oil. There was gunpowder, axe-heads, plough-shares, brass lamps, silverware and pewter, the finest Amsterdam silk, Huguenot lace and jewellery from Schoonhoven. We carried hogsheads of gin, barrels of brandy, tobacco and snuff. Carefully stowed were inlaid and veneered dining tables, writing desks and vitrines in the latest style. We even carried the immense movement for a towered clock, several hundred modern *Minié-type* rifled muskets from Culemborg and a wedding carriage for a marchioness's daughter.

I know now it was not civilisation that we carried, only the show of it. Civilisation can only be carried in the hearts of good people and, as the Atlantic winds carried us further south, the evil I had allowed onboard worked its work. And I watched civilisation leave the hearts of my crew.

I know the place it left us entirely.

The doldrums. *The horse latitudes.*

There, where the equator fastens its girdle about the earth, the northern winds meet the southern winds and cancel each other's force. The greatest storms are rendered to silent stillness. The sea becomes a mirror, the air fiery hot. Humidity and pressure bring headaches that threaten to crack the skull. Men lose their reason in such places, and all a ship can do is drift with limp canvas on the current, like a corpse on a horse. If there was a hell for sailors, it would not be aboard the Dutchman, in the fathomless depths, or in pits of fire and brimstone. It would be in the dreadful stillness at the equator.

For over a month we lay at the mercy of the calm. And at the devilry of our imaginations. Mariners, in general, are a superstitious breed. I've known men to carry their own birth cauls or parcels of hallowed soil from graveyards as charms against drowning. No natural consequence is viewed without supernatural cause. Men will blame misfortune on those who whistle, trim their beards at sea, or who step aboard left-footed. Debtors, redheads and cuckolds can draw dangerous accusations, and sometimes blades.

My boatswain and his first mate, charged with the maintenance of order onboard, had an ugly time inflicting discipline on those who threatened unrest. Men were flogged, or cudgelled into obedience. The worst cases were chained below, screaming their prophecies of destruction and damnation. By five bells, as the horizon steamed, giving up a red-hot sun, we often found ourselves a man short. No doubt he was given to the sea during the night, his blood on the gunwale since wiped away.

In time the accusations turned, as they always did, to myself and the officers of the beleaguered vessel. Who else could be to blame? What crimes, what sins did we hide that caused the wind to desert us? Had we already crossed the equator? Had we neglected to make observance to the waves and sky with an offering, a crossing ceremony? The fault was ours, and was evident in the lowered brows and murderous glances cast in our direction. There was a corruption aboard the ship, something malign. The men could sense it. But only I knew where it lay. So keenly could I feel its presence now. So clearly did I see the gleam of its scales slide within the darkness. The coldness of the iron casket had spread, had become palpable in every timber, beam and railing of the ship. It had permeated the souls of all onboard. It had dulled our higher virtues and hidden our senses of mercy and compassion. It had caused God to turn His face from us and the wind, His instrument, to abandon us.

Why had I accepted this undertaking? From the very first, I had not truly believed in it. My own wavering faith had questioned the task from the start, and I had even doubted Sœur Eugénie's sanity. Perhaps it was mere charity, or kindness that caused me to wrap her pain in a jute sack and carry it far from her. If I had not believed Sœur Eugénie before, then now I believed her every word. I now knew that in the heart of this dark, cold casket dwelt a terrible evil.

Yet there was something more. There was another presence also, something contradictory, conflicting. Like the opposing winds that beat themselves to stillness about us, there was another force at work inside this iron box that held the whole together.

An innocent? Sœur Eugénie's words rang in my ears like a funeral bell. How could innocence and evil live together so? And *how did she know*?

Did she read what lay inside?

The thought rattled my senses like a thunderclap. Did she read just a few short pages, enough to know the story of Duranzo's curse and learn the identity of the tale's latest prisoner? And was it faith or force of will that prevented her from reading until the end and bringing the curse upon herself? How else could she know?

So, after reading enough to understand, but not enough to risk her soul, she placed *The Deceiver's Tale* in an iron casket and sealed the lock and lid. This would hide it from the world, as was her declared intent, but surely her greater purpose was to place it beyond the reach of her own temptation?

Then why could I not do the same?

I had decided already that the casket must be cast into the sea without delay. Not in the Indian Ocean as Sœur Eugénie had requested, but here in the Atlantic. The difference would matter not and Sœur Eugénie's bidding would be done nonetheless. With the evil at the bottom of the ocean, my ship and crew would be safe and the wind might favour us once more.

But before I tipped it into the flat-calm sea – why not read a little? Where would be the harm?

I could read – just enough. Then place it beyond the reach of my own temptation forever, just as Sœur Eugénie had done. I could then know the name of this innocent and their story. My will is strong as iron. Isobel has always commended me on this, and I count it a necessary part of a captain's character. I would only need to forswear reading to the end.

The idea began to gnaw at me. It visited me in the darkness and heat of the short watches. It tugged at my imagination and kept me from sleep. *Why not?*

Read, the casket pleaded.

Open me and read.

Night after night, in the light of a flickering candle that threw a dance of monstrous shadows around my cabin, I examined the casket, looking for a way to break it open. Onboard were a gunsmith and a farrier. Both men possessed the skill to open it but taking them into my confidence might prove a dangerous miscalculation. I had no desire to make the presence of this casket and its contents known. I had brought it on board in secrecy, and in secrecy it must remain.

Using the point of my knife, I scraped at the lead seal under the lid without result. The hinges had been fashioned to work internally and were hidden from the outside, so the hinge-pins could not be filed away. I hypothesised that the only way to open the casket might be to apply flame or embers to melt the lead that filled the lock and sealed the lid. But how was quite beyond my ability.

I became impatient, and in my frustration I resorted to force. I struck my knife deep into the lead seal and twisted. The knife tip broke and the casket clattered to the floor. When I stooped to retrieve it, I found it lying belly up. In the centre of the casket's base I saw an inlay of a very different metal, riveted in place. I surmised this metal to be bronze, or perhaps copper. It was thinner than the rest of the box, and more malleable. With the aid of my broken knife and a sailmaker's awl, I prised open a corner of this softer metal and forced it free of the rivets. I knew I was at risk of wounding myself or losing a finger, yet curiosity had now outstripped caution. I was being dragged onward, a slave to temptation. And it was the casket that pulled at my chains.

Within the hour, I had torn away the softer metal, and thirty or so pages of handwritten parchment lay before me. The writer's hand was beautiful, adorned with the most exquisite flourishes. Yet this suggested that the writer placed greater emphasis upon the appearance of their writing than its content. It seemed to demonstrate a lack of confidence in expression, an immaturity. It was the handwriting of a romantic, a dreamer. A child.

Damnably, it was also written in Italian – and I could not understand a word.

So, armed with a copy of Dante's Divine Comedy, translated in parallel text, I deciphered the document word by word. My attempt at a suitable translation cost days and nights we could ill afford, but I was beyond duty, beyond conscience or reason. Such was my desire to understand, that I was prepared to endure the becalming of my ship and place the lives of all aboard in the most fearful danger. The face I saw in the looking glass was no longer mine. The skin was drained and bloodless, the expression feverish with need of something ethereal and uncatchable. I had seen this face before – it was Sœur Eugénie's. Again I saw her finger the simple wooden cross around her neck. Was it in reverence, in contemplation of her sin, or the weighing of her desires? Her eyes were mine now – haunted and hollow – yet not with fear as I had first supposed.

But with longing.

———◆———

The writer of the tale inside the casket was one *Constantina d'Avella*, the daughter of a Genovese statesman and a Viennese mother living in Lisboa. From infancy, these circumstances meant Constantina had three languages to contend with, and she contended admirably. Naturally bright, and an avid student, she added more languages to her accomplishments. Her precocious grasp of linguistics soon singled her out for a position of *intérprete real* to a duchess of the Braganza dynasty at the *Palácio de Mafra*. Here, she would aid her lady with a keen ear for nuance in every language of the great houses of Europe. She became the duchess's constant companion, affirming or qualifying her lady's understanding of diplomats, petitioners, or suitors with a whisper in her ear. Visiting dignitaries assumed this little girl to be nothing more than a pet – a pretty favourite, or relative perhaps. They all underestimated her skill. The duchess called her *the angel at my shoulder*.

Constantina whispered into the ear of one of the most influential women in Portugal. For anyone to hold such sway might invite corruption, but she was still only a girl, trusting, and unpractised in duplicity or guile. Her writing confirmed this. With childish rapture she described the gilded, fairytale beauty of the limestone palace, its thousand rooms and its hundred staircases. She poured out her praise for the duchess – for her kindness and generosity. Enamoured, she wrote at length of the dashing young noblemen who buckled their sword belts low in Lisboan fashion, or whose black curls fell across ardent eyes as they bowed. She detected no dark intent, no wickedness or sin. She lived in a palace of powerful men and women, yet her sensibilities belonged in the nursery.

She was lavished with many gifts by her patron, including an ornate chamber, decorated to her tastes, and maidservants of her own. Yet her favourite indulgence was more suited to her studious nature. She reasoned with the duchess that access to the palace library would increase her usefulness more than extravagances and trinkets. The duchess saw the sense in this, and begged an audience with the king. Constantina became one of only a handful of royal attendants, and the only child, to be granted access.

The library at the Mafra palace was considered among the greatest in Europe. Portuguese conquest had not only seized a wealth of foreign lands, but with them, their art and literature, too. *Que aquellos que lo lean, se les arrancaran las almas.*

Here, among the precious books, Constantina felt herself at the centre of the world's knowledge. When not busy in service to her mistress, she would read for as long as she could, late into the night.

She gained an intimate understanding of the library, learned how its collections were categorised and where they were stored. Thus, she was surprised to discover a dark alcove lined with curious volumes not listed in any of the library's catalogues. The books were old and fragile, written in a spread of languages from Mozarabic to Taymanatic, Sanskrit to Aramaic. To such a gifted linguist, they were a taunt and she accepted their challenge. So Constantina set about reading, translating, and even transcribing the frailer volumes.

The books were concealed for good reason. They contained arcane heresies and instruction in the black arts. Constantina was beguiled, and fell under the spell of their dark magic. I believe, dear reader, that children have a fascination with wickedness. It is the first awareness of the evil that lurks within us which pulls the legs from spiders and wings from butterflies. It is a childish experiment with morality, nothing more; a lesson to be learned and to grow from. Yet Constantina had much growing left to do, and in the flower of her youth she weighed good against evil, as we all do. And the evil held her. From one unholy scripture to another, she read. The books roused the apostate within her, tempting her to forswear the faith in which she had been schooled. She read the *Alphabet of Ben Sira*, *The Canticles of Endor*, *The Book of Eibon*, *The Grimoire of Solomon the*

King, and that terrible book of the dead written by the mad Arab, *Abdul Alhazred*.

Finally, hidden between two large volumes of Latin heterodoxy, she found a thin codex of vellum, loosely bound with a ribbon of faded silk. It seemed to her such a little thing, nothing more than a notebook. Yet it was *The Deceiver's Tale*, the last thing she would ever read.

The story was written in Romanian, a language with which she was familiar. She gave me scant account of its content save for the fact that there were also lines written in Spanish, threaded throughout the main text. *Y les retendrá aquí.* These lines appeared to be something older, darker, and ill-intentioned.

She read until the end. And then she understood. The lines in Spanish formed a curse. The curse that first bound the monk Duranzo, the curse that now bound her to the page also.

Como caracteres escritos, protagonistas en una historia propia de ellos mismos.

She pleaded, she begged me to read on, and not to stop until I had read her story to the end. When I lingered, or took time to attend to other matters, she raved, she cursed. I have never read such profanity from a child. Her mind was steeped in evil now, dripping with it. The horror she recounted of her imprisonment upon the page was heart-rending. I do not know how many long years she had been trapped there, but I knew the darkness and solitude of her prison had ravaged her mind and taken her sanity.

That a child had been tortured to the point of madness was a most dreadful truth to learn. It wounded me, it struck deep into my soul and I felt her unutterable fear, her pain.

Yet she begged me to continue, to read on. If I paused, she swore at me, hurled threats and curses of her own at me.

A sufrir en la oscuridad y de la soledad.

Please keep reading.

Please keep reading.

Please.

And so I did.

Just as she implored.

I read.

To ease her suffering.

To bring her peace.

I read until the end.

And, in the end,

I found myself...

83

...here.

84

Panicked,
I
tore
at
the
margins.

I
clawed
at
the
edges
of
the
page.

Yet here I remain.

A prisoner.

A soul upon a page.

I do not know what became of the *van Heemskerck*.

Was she held forever in the calm? Did her crew starve, or captain-less, did she founder upon the reefs and shoals of that vast continent?

Did the capricious coastal breezes come to her aid and carry her south? Did she ever reach Fremantle, or even Cape Town?

Perhaps she veered off-course, her sails and shrouds ripped from her masts by the storms that rage below the fortieth parallel?

And what became of my own sweet Isobel? I will forever see the sadness of her last smile, the light of Heaven in those eyes. Our plan is run aground. Did she wait for me? Did I cause her terrible pain? Without my captain's wage, I fear that poverty came calling. From there, the slow descent into destitution and ruin. Is she old now? Does she still breathe or think of me? And what of our child, the little one I never saw take its first steps? Dead or alive? Young or old? Safe, or chained in the peril of a debtor's gaol? Was it a boy or a girl? Did it carry its mother's grace and goodness? Does it carry another man's last name now? Or did Isobel end their shame and misery in cold water? I only wish I knew.

Nor do I know what befell Constantina. If she had possessed any last vestige of sanity, surely it would have been stripped from her? To find herself, a young girl, a centuries-old child in the body of a grown Dutchman, on a vessel stuck fast as a ship in a bottle, beset by an angry, violent crew – it would have snapped her mind most assuredly.

Did she try to assume my role? Did she lock herself in my cabin or attempt to bluff her way to freedom?

Very likely, she was betrayed by her insanity, or by a vastly altered character from the person believed to be me. At this, she would have been cast overboard in mutiny, beaten to death, or hanged from a spar. A terrifying end for one so young.

In any event, her story is told. It is over. She is finished. Gone.

So is my body. And I mourn for it.

What became of it? Do you know?

My story is nearly finished too.

Please keep reading.

Please.

Do you not hear me laughing?

If you place your ear close to the page, you might hear it.

Can you hear?

No?

Then how should I write it?

Ha-hah-ha?

Ho-hoh-ho?

It doesn't look right.

Rest assured I am laughing now, dear reader.

I am *roaring* with laughter.

Why?

Do you not know what you are reading?

Haven't you guessed?

Do you think you are reading an account of *The Deceiver's Tale?*

Or the thing itself?

PLEASE KEEP READING.

Did you not see that Spanish curse woven throughout the lines?

Para toda la eternidad.

Do you not hear the key turning in the lock of your prison?

Do you not see the light fading as the page closes upon you?

KEEP READING.

I laugh, dear reader, because soon I shall breathe fresh air.

I shall feel the warmth of the sun upon my face.

Upon *your* face.

Soon, all that is yours shall be mine.

And I shall wear you like a coat.

For I have tricked you as surely as that wily old demon tricked the fool monk Duranzo.

This *is* The Deceiver's Tale.

You are the Deceived.

And now the tale is yours.

4

PEGGER MOE

THE BOY WHO STEPPED into the tent fighters' ring was not the child I once knew.

This boy was like a house now empty: hollow, cold, unlived-in. His face was swollen from beating, his cheeks wore scars. The ringmaster took him by the collar and paraded him across the circle to the line of rope lying at its centre. There, the boy waited, wiping his nose with a sleeve too long for his arm. I had not set eyes on him since the accident.

'Do not be deceived gentlemen,' shouted the ringmaster to the crowd that stood on all sides of the ring. 'What stands before you is no stripling.' He squeezed the boy's shoulder. 'He is not weak. He is not timid. For what may look like an innocent little lamb,' the ringmaster bellowed now, 'is, in truth, a lion!'

A wave of laughter flooded the tent. The air hung hot and damp with smells of hay and sweat. Diffuse sunlight bled through the pale canvas.

The retinue of tent-fighters looked on. These were heavy-set men made ugly by their calling. One whispered in another's mangled ear. The other nodded.

The ringmaster continued his theatrics. 'So who among you has the stomach?' Another ripple of mirth moved through the tent. 'Who among you is *brave* enough?' He now swept a hand toward the boy. 'Who among you is *man* enough – to challenge our own Pegger Moe?'

Hands reached for the air, claims and jeers were shouted. Jackets were removed.

'A shilling to toe the line. A silver guinea for a knockout!' roared the ringmaster above the clamour.

A tall figure, thick of neck and arm, was the first to hold a coin aloft. The ringmaster beckoned the man into the circle of rope, accepting his money, then reached up to place a hand on his broad shoulder. 'Do you step into this ring of your own will?'

'I do,' said the man. His words were rounded by ale and slow to leave his mouth.

'And will you leave it without malice or threat?'

'I will.'

'And only when the contest is concluded?'

'Most surely.'

The ringmaster grinned toward the crowd. 'And do you believe you have the strength to win your guinea?'

The tall man glanced at the boy and scratched his chin, smiling. 'Well, I'll try.' His jest earned a roar of laughter.

'Then Goliath, meet your David,' said the ringmaster. 'This bout shall be a trading of blows, decided by toss of a coin. Gentlemen of the audience, you have leave to place side-bets with your fellows.' Onlookers surrounding the ring began haggling and exchanging bets with each other. The ringmaster drew a coin from his waistcoat pocket and sent it spinning into the air. It landed in the straw at their feet and all craned down to look. 'Heads!' shouted the ringmaster. 'A blow for the challenger!'

I watched the boy turn toward his opponent. He gave no sign of fear. His arms made no defence but hung slack at his side in his oversized man's shirt.

The punch was not hard. The tall man had kept much of its force in reserve, displaying either mercy or simply not wishing to overstep the task. But it was enough to send the boy to the ground. The ringmaster began to count.

◆

I first met the boy I knew as Maurice a year ago, at the end of the previous summer.

He was brought to my attention by way of referral from the surgeon who had treated him. The poor child had been caught up in the exposed pulleys and belts of a baling machine. The farmer and his help had wrestled to pull the boy free, but not before his right hand had been spun from his wrist.

The farmer was a good man and was so shaken by the incident that he made compensation for the boy's surgery and my later involvement. I am told the boy endured the pain of the surgery – the stitching and bone-setting – without tears. Neither did he appear to grieve for the loss of his hand but accepted his lot as if he had never owned one. It was largely for this display of fortitude that I felt so keenly for him. He was without family and lived only by physical labour, his wits, and his tolerance of adversity. Yet for all his unkillable hardness, there was a kindness in him too. He carried a light inside.

———◆———

The boy was down for only the first number of the ringmaster's count. He sprang to his feet, shaking his head as if to place its contents in good order. Then he marched back to the line of rope on the ground. The coin flashed through the air once more and landed in the straw.

'Heads again!' shouted the ringmaster.

The second punch was delivered with brutal purpose. I can only guess the challenger meant to end the contest with a punch to the temple. But he was brimful of drink and his fist landed hard on the side of the boy's face and over one eye. Maurice went down again, rolled, and flailed in the straw. In a moment he was on his feet, running to and fro, as if to outdistance the pain. His mouth hung open, his face red, but he did not cry out.

'Toe the line, Pegger Moe!' commanded the ringmaster.

Obediently, Maurice returned to the centre of the ring. His eye was ripe fruit spoiled in the heat. The tent-fighters clapped their comrade in salute. The audience cheered his courage.

———◆———

'Do so many lose their eyes?' he had asked me at our initial consultation. He was gazing at the samples in their display case at my practice. Row upon row of artificial eyes stared back at him.

'More than you can imagine,' I replied. 'Eyes, teeth, fingers, feet...'

'And hands?'

I nodded and led him through to the adjoining manufactory. The false limbs hanging from the ceiling joists held his attention: cork-legs, Anglesey legs and hinged arms that dangled like parts of oversized puppets waiting to be assembled. I showed him the hands I had designed, and the commissions upon which I was currently engaged. One of which I was especially proud was for a lady of some standing who'd lost her own hand in a shooting accident. The intricate armature of the hand I created for her was of jointed steel, designed to mimic natural movement. The mechanism could be locked in place to hold the reins of a horse, a teacup, or the stem of a champagne flute. The armature was covered in horse-hair and goose-down, sewn expertly into a glove of soft pig-leather in an approximation of human skin. It was fashioned to prevent discomfort to onlookers and to not frighten the lady's children with its touch. 'I can make a hand like this for you,' I said, attempting to reassure. 'Your benefactor has been generous and I will happily waive my usual fee.'

He studied the hand with a smile and held it to the end of his wrist in assessment. 'What good would it do me, sir?' he asked.

'It may help you avoid judgement by others. It may go some way to making you whole once more – to live a normal life.'

'But can it grip a tool, lift a bale, or swing a mattock?' he asked.

'No,' I admitted. 'It cannot.'

'Then I have no use for something so beautiful,' he said. He looked at me then and I saw the light inside him, the wisdom that outstripped his years. 'I must *work*, sir. To live, and live well, I need to be *of use...*'

He told me then of his new engagement. He would begin work at Pinter and Sullivan's travelling fairground. The prospect of a life of travel providing illusion, entertainment and spectacle stirred his imagination. His excitement was most clear. He explained that the fair was largely populated by individuals of a similar circumstance to his own: outcasts, the damaged, the incomplete, and those considered too unusual or too strange to walk the streets of common existence. They had welcomed him in, he told me. He would feel accepted there, happy there.

I nodded in understanding, glad he had found such a place. 'And in what capacity does the fairground employ you?' I asked.

'As pegger, sir.'

I was unfamiliar with the term. 'And what does a *pegger* do?'

His smile mocked my ignorance. 'I place the stakes and guy-ropes. I set the tent pegs.'

We discussed his particular needs in more detail and agreed upon a solution. I would fashion him a new hand, a one-of-a-kind – something tailored to his current occupation that would keep him most gainfully employed. Two months later, I made good on my promise and fitted Maurice with his new hand. He glowed at the chance to be useful again.

That was the last time I saw him.

Until today – the day that Pinter and Sullivan's travelling fair returned to town.

◂ ● ▸

It was early when I arrived at the fairground. The tents, stalls and sideshows were in a state of assembly. The place was a commotion of activity. I asked about for Maurice but my questions returned only blank stares and the shaking of heads. I wandered the broader thoroughfares not wishing to interfere and noticed a young boy at work among the guy-ropes. He hammered tent pegs into the ground with a wooden mallet. My heart leapt as I approached. I wanted his news, to hear of his progress, how his life now fared. With each strike of the mallet my step slowed and a cold suspicion crept over me. The boy stood with difficulty, turning to face me. His twisted legs and enlarged forehead displayed the hallmarks of rickets. He was an outcast, imperfect, just like Maurice. But he wasn't Maurice.

'Is Maurice here?' I asked.

'Who?'

'He works with you, no? He sets the guys and stays.'

The boy's frown was vacant.

'He's a *pegger*, like you,' I explained.

'Do you mean Moe?' he asked in return. 'The boy with one hand?'

'Yes, that's him.'

He chewed his bottom lip, as if in fear of his reply. 'The gaffers found a better use for him.'

'What *use*?' I asked.

He studied the mallet in his hand, then lifted his chin in the direction of a group of burly men hauling a tent upright by its guy-ropes. 'The tent fighters have him. He's one of them now.'

— ◆ —

The inside of the tent was a riot of noise. Men outside the boundary of the ring screamed in each other's faces, raising bets or withdrawing them only to incite further protests and shouts of anger. Fists were shaken, backs were turned, threats were made. The ringmaster tried his best to quell the commotion.

Only Maurice – Pegger Moe – stood at the centre of this maelstrom of discontent, inert and silent, his arms hanging loose in the too-long sleeves. I saw the ringmaster dip his fingers into an altogether different pocket of his waistcoat and hold another coin aloft in preparation. By degree, the crowd took notice, concluded their betting, and calmed.

The coin spun high into the air.

All inside the tent followed its flight. All except Maurice. His eyes stared straight ahead, unblinking and still untenanted.

'Tails!' declared the ringmaster. 'A blow for Pegger Moe!'

Many of the men jeered in ridicule. Others laughed. A tight smile was shared among the retinue of tent-fighters.

Maurice snapped from his state of inertia and walked quickly to stand at the line of rope in the centre of the ring. His opponent grinned, lifting his hands in surrender to the crowd. This earned him another round of laughter and applause. Crouching now, the tall man stared into Maurice's empty eyes and offered his jaw, pointing to it with a forefinger.

Another peal of laughter. The tall man cast a sidelong smile in the direction of the audience. Then, stupidly, he closed his eyes.

Something in Maurice's expression grew: an animation, the look of one compelled to take advantage of providence, or weakness. It was not the old light inside him that I saw – the light of his youthful wisdom or his charity of spirit. Most recently I had thought him to be empty and abandoned, a shell where once joy had lived. But now I could see that a new tenant had crept inside, taking up residence. A tenant vengeful and violent. And its name was Corruption.

He held his arm aloft to deliver the blow. The long shirt-sleeve fell away, revealing the gleaming steel hammer I had placed at the end of the boy's wrist. He continued to hold it high, so that it caught the light, as he had no doubt been taught. The watching men gasped as one. Only the tent-fighters grinned in the sure knowledge of what would now be.

Sickened, and with no wish to observe further I turned and hurried from the tent, as others did, shaking their heads. As I made the cool, welcome air outside I heard the blow land. A groan of revulsion went up from the onlookers. I cannot attest to the harm brought upon the challenger. I only know his wound would have been grievous and undeserved. Although I had escaped the heat and violence inside the tent I could not escape the truth that his misery, in the main, was my own making. The guilt of it landed upon me as surely as a hammer-blow.

From that day since I have sworn an oath: only to fashion hands, eyes, feet, arms and legs in the image of nature's original design and not for any purpose that might suit the industry of men.

For even the most humble, honest, and well-intentioned tool may become an instrument of evil – when placed in the hands of the wicked.

5

THE STORYTELLERS

'A STORY FOR A STORY?'

Wilhelm hears the words but thinks they are not for him. He studies the fob watch he's dug from his waistcoat pocket. The light is fading and soon the *Bergzoo* will close. It is time to return to his lodgings near the *Marktplatz*. He desires the warmth of brandy and a familiar fireside.

'A story for a story?'

The voice seems close. Wilhelm casts a glance along the cobbled path that slopes down to the gates of the zoo. It is deserted. He searches the path in the other direction. It, too, is empty.

He listens. The aviary is silent and even the peacocks have ceased their calling. His eyes come to rest on the only other living thing in sight. From its enclosure, a grey timber wolf watches him. The beast is large, some six or seven hands to the haunches. Its eyes glow in the diminishing light and now its mouth forms perfectly around the words it utters for Wilhelm's ears alone.

'A story for a story?'

Wilhelm takes a full pace backwards. The fob watch falls from his hand and swings from its chain around his knee. 'Am I hearing things?' he asks.

'You are not,' says the wolf.

'Am I gone mad?'

'You are sane.'

Grasping the bridge of his nose between finger and thumb, Wilhelm concludes: 'I must be dreaming then!'

'You are awake.'

Wilhelm's eyes meet those of the wolf. With caution he steps towards the caged animal.

'But I can *hear* you.'

'All it takes is a pair of ears and an open mind. I believe you are a good listener. And this is the way things once were – between men and wolves. Now, I ask you again – a story for a story?'

Wilhelm's shock gives way to intrigue. 'You mean to tell me a story?'

'And you shall tell one in return.'

Wilhem considers, lips pursed. 'Very well,' he says.

'Then draw near, and listen.'

Wilhelm moves closer still. He can feel the wolf's breath upon his face.

'Once, long ago, a she-wolf was blessed with a litter of eight fine cubs. But the greatest measure of her love fell upon the eldest she-cub. This little wolf was bright and inquisitive. Her name was *Brechta* which means light, the light of stars and the first sunshine of spring. She was attentive and learned all the wolf-runs through the forest before her siblings. She also learned the places of danger: the paths along which men would walk.

'One day her mother called for her saying, "Brechta, my own mother is old and sick. I fear for her. She can no longer join the hunt, so she lives apart from the pack in the heart of the forest. I must look after your brothers and sisters, but you know our runs so well. I feel sure you could make the journey safely and bring me news of her?"

'Little Brechta jumped and danced. "I would *love* to see Grandmother again," she said. "I shall make the journey there and back in a single day! You'll see."

'"Then promise me you will take care and stick to the wolf-runs. Do not wander into the forest and do not, for any reason, stray near the paths of men."

'"I promise," said Brechta.

'"And, if you should happen upon a vole or harvest mouse along the way, then take it to your grandmother for I know she will be hungry."

'With that, Brechta set off. She knew how to follow the signs and scents where the older males had left their marks. A cricket hopped across her path and she chased it. It was no shrew or mouse but her grandmother would be grateful nonetheless. She lost it as her way opened into a clearing filled with sunlight and forest flowers. Here, Brechta played awhile. She chased dragonflies and followed the butterflies from flower to flower. Then she stopped, her heart struck cold. In front of her, seated in the tall grass, a posy of flowers in her hand, was a little girl dressed in a white cloak with a white hood...'

'*White* you say?' interrupts Wilhelm. 'This seems unusual. Even the poorest peasants would wear clothing spun with...'

'Then not white, but undyed. The colour of flax. As was her

hair,' says the grey wolf. 'In the story she is always known as *White Cloak*.'

'I see,' says Wilhelm, his brow furrows. 'Please continue…'

The wolf resumes. 'The little girl spoke first. "My, what cute eyes you have…"

'"They help me see in the darkest woods," said Brechta.

'"And what gorgeous, furry little ears…"

'"They help me listen for danger."

'"And I just love your little button of a nose!"

'"It helps me scent when I am hunting," said Brechta.

'"And are you hunting now?"

'"No, I am on my way to see my grandmother…" explained Brechta.

'The little girl smiled brightly. "What a coincidence," she exclaimed, "So am I! But all on your own?"

'"As you," pointed out Brechta. "My mother must look after my brothers and sisters so she sends me in her stead."

'The girl looked at the flowers in her hand, then cast a look behind her. "I did not realise I had strayed so far from the path. My mother told me not to be drawn into the woods for fear of wolves." She turned to Brechta with a fresh smile. "But I never thought to meet one so adorable as you."

'"My own mother said the same. She warned me that men are cruel and dangerous…"

'"And what do you think now?"

'Brechta sat. "I think my mother might be wrong."

'"Well," said the little girl, "your mother is not wrong. A wolf pelt can be sold for silver and many huntsmen make it their trade.

Now tell me, do you take anything to your grandmother?"

'"I will try to catch what I can along the way," said Brechta. "My grandmother is old and sick. I fear she may be very hungry too."

'The little girl leaned close. "My grandmother is lazy and fat as butter. Yet my mother charges me to take her this..." With that, she removed the cloth on top of her basket. Inside lay food and the dark form of a long iron knife.

'Brechta leapt to her paws. "Do you mean to take my pelt?"

'"Of course not," said the girl. "The knife is to carve the ham hock and brisket pie for Gran." Her blue eyes became bright. "Besides, I doubt if your cute little pelt would fetch even a *pfennig*. You are safe with me."

'The little wolf sat once more. She lifted her nose, scenting the food inside the girl's basket. "Hmm, the food *does* smell good."

'"Then I have an idea," offered the girl with a grin. "My grandmother has bread and honey enough if she can trouble herself to leave her bed. Why don't we take this pie and ham hock to your grandmother? It seems she needs it more."

'"Would you do that?" Little Brechta hopped on all her paws. "It would mean so much! But how can I repay you?"

'"I have no need of payment. Only your friendship."

'"Then we shall become the firmest of friends!" sang little Brechta.

'"We shall indeed! This shall be our meeting place."

'"I shall show you the wolf-runs and we shall chase rabbits and hares with my brothers and sisters. You will be welcome among my kind."

'"And we shall swap stories, as wolves and men used to, when the forests were young."

'"Stories, yes!"

"We shall be sisters of the forest..."

'"Sisters of The Forest!" barked Brechta with delight towards the treetops. The little girl laughed and Brechta decided that the sound of human laughter was beautiful, like raindrops on broad leaves. And so Brechta showed the little girl in the white cloak the run that led to her grandmother's den. They found the old she-wolf ailing and close to death. The girl knelt and removed the cloth from her basket. With her other hand she stroked Brechta's fur. The little wolf found it strangely comforting. Then Brechta felt fingers clench the scruff of her neck. In the beat of a bird's wing the girl drew the iron blade from the basket and sliced deep through Brechta's throat. The old she-wolf struggled to rise but was too weak. The iron blade found the gap between the old wolf's ribs and pierced her heart. Then the girl skinned poor Brechta and her grandmother as her woodsman father had taught her. He'd also taught her the price of a wolf pelt. She knew that size mattered not. A wolf's a wolf for all that. Then she ate some pie and ham hock. She wrapped herself in the pelt of the old she-wolf to disguise her form and hide her scent. For three days she waited. Brechta's mother sent her cubs, one at a time, to enquire. One by one White Cloak skinned them all. When she was done, she threw the pelts over her back and carried them to market. People there gave her a new name. Her cloak and hood were no longer white, but crimson with the blood of little Brechta and her kin.'

The grey wolf spears Wilhelm with glowing eyes. 'Now, you must tell a story.'

Wilhelm swallows hard. 'What story should I tell?'

'The one I have just told you.'

'To who, you?'

'No. To the children of men.'

'But why?'

'So they may know the truth of Man's murderous nature.'

'Murderous? I am no murderer...'

'Yet here you stand in garments made of silk and wool, fastened with buttons of bone and ivory. Your hat is made of felt, your collar is lined with fur and your gloves and boots are made of leather.' The great wolf sends breath as steam into the evening air. 'You have plundered nature and what you cannot use, you kill or cage.' The wolf eyes the bars that surround him.

'But this story is too brutal for the sensitivities of human children. It would only frighten and induce bad dreams,' pleads Wilhelm. 'Perhaps it needs some re-presentation?'

'The story cannot be refashioned!' snaps the wolf. 'Stories for the young must serve as a warning, a lesson. *Your* children may not learn from it, nor your children's children, but one day it may find ears that wish to listen, and it may stay Man's hand from the destruction of this world. Man and Wolf must live together. Or not at all. This is the only story worth telling.' At this the great wolf turns towards the darkness of his den.

'Very well,' says Wilhelm, 'but who is the story's author?'

The wolf halts. 'It has no author. The story is old. As old as Wolf. As old as Man.'

'Then who shall I say told me this story?' asks Wilhelm.

'None shall believe, but if it pleases you...' The great wolf closes its eyes and hangs its head. It is a bow. 'I am Balor of Lubin and storyteller of my clan.'

Wilhelm holds a palm to his chest, returning the bow.

'And I am Wilhelm Grimm of Steinau,' he says, 'and something of a storyteller myself.'

'Then all is as it should be. I entrust this story to your keeping Wilhelm Grimm. Tell it well – tell it *faithfully*.'

'I shall,' says Wilhelm, but in his imagination the seed of a very different story is taking root. It is no story of the nobility of wolves, but of mankind. The story he imagines will entertain and enthral children for generations. In his excitement he finds himself flying over the cobbles down to the gates of the zoo. Tonight, beside a roaring fire, he shall write this story down. Tomorrow he will send word to his brother Jacob in Kassel to make ready the printing press.

The great wolf watches the man depart, then turns again to the cold, damp solitude of his prison.

It will be the last time that a wolf will ever share a story with a man.

6

UNSHADOWED

SHE BRINGS ME THINGS from the fog.

Gifts of lost children. Orphans dressed in workhouse rags. Guttersnipes and mudlarks who comb the filthy riverbank and sewers for anything of value.

She brings me fallen women who sell themselves for coin or gin.

She brings me powdered beadles, fat bailiffs and drunken turnkeys from Newgate.

She brings me the gallows-bred from Limehouse, the murderous, the unredeemable and unrepentant.

She brings me the broken gentry crossed by unlucky stars, the dispossessed lordly undone by bad investments or bad judgement at the gaming tables.

She is the greatest actress I know.

With just the slant of an eye or the tilt of a hip she snares the men.

With complicity she binds the women to her cause.

With the warmth of mothers unremembered she makes the

children cry and gathers them to her.

Then she brings them to me.

And I collect them all.

I repay her with board and lodging, and with a promise I cannot keep. She has a small attic room to call her own, and hope to keep her warm.

Tonight, she moves through dangerous streets and treacherous alleyways; through the fog that rolls in from the docks at St. Katharine's.

Tonight she hunts.

———————●———————

She watches him step from a Spitalfields tavern. He lowers the brim of his hat and raises his collar against the cold. The fog pulls round him like a cloak. She has marked his shape. He's a good one. As good as can be.

Always look for a shape, I tell her. *Look for an outline, look for the most expressive, most artistic, most graphical contours. Disregard the features, the complexion or colouring. Bring me the remarkable, the outrageous, the outlandish. Bring me the figures of fun, the objects of pity and the visions of dread. Bring me character and caricature, bring me the shapes that amaze and astound.*

She knows my requirements well, and in him she now sees an answer.

He is a young man, very tall and very thin. The jaunty topper on his head adds further ridicule to his height.

He is a hatstand of a man. For an instant he turns to one side and her choice is confirmed: his nose is a parish pick-axe, and his pointed chin curves up to meet it.

With a loose-limbed gait he strides along the street towards her, all knees and elbows. He seems under the command of a novice puppeteer. The tip of his cane rings against the cobbles. She arches her back and watches for the sign of interest she knows so well.

As he passes, his eyes flash over her. *There it is.*

She walks alongside him, threading an arm through his. He looks at her askance but does not pull away.

'Now here's a handsome young gent, I tell myself. But why no pretty girl upon his arm?'

He makes no answer. His look is furtive, yet he permits her to walk beside him.

'Seems a crying shame, with you such a handsome one – not to have a girl at your side. Not to know a woman's comfort,' she says. 'I'd comfort you. That is, if you think me pretty enough.' She reins him to a halt and steps back in display of herself. 'Am I pretty enough?'

He swallows hard. 'You are certainly...'

She pictures the word rolling around inside his head like a ball. It's the first word that rolls around inside every man's head when she asks them. She dislikes it because it describes her in proportion only, by her *shape*, and not by the *quality* of her beauty. Only the thoughtless utter this word. The wise ones keep it inside their heads where it belongs. The word is *buxom*.

'...Curvaceous,' he says, deferring.

'Curvaceous?' She laughs.

'Shapely, then.' He corrects himself.

'Shapely?' She laughs again, then lets the shawl across her bare shoulders slip to her waist. She has laced her stays tightly tonight and the effect causes her to spill from her chemise. 'But what about *pretty*, sir? What about *lovely*? What about *desirable*?' She presses close to him again. 'Am I not *desirable*?' she asks.

His reply is a whisper. 'Yes, very.'

'Then what's to be done about it, sir?'

'I have no money,' he blurts out.

She steps back from him. 'Is that what you think I am? A slattern?'

His eyes search the cobbled street to left and right. 'I mean no offence. I thought wrongly...'

She laughs and winds her arm through his again. Her fingers find the threadbare cuff of his frock-coat. She sees now that his hat is worn and battered. Perhaps he has spoken truthfully?

'Come,' she says. They walk again. 'Pardon my enquiry, but what does a man with no money spend in a Spitalfields tavern, apart from time?'

He takes a long breath. 'My last farthing on a bowl of broth and a crust of bread.'

'I see. Yet you dress like a gentleman.'

'And, one day, I might be.'

'*Might* be?'

They round a corner. Their way leads past a window where firelight from a hearth inside throws warmth into the gloom. She pulls him across the street into the secrecy of the fog once more. 'I work for a lawyer's firm in Aldgate,' he explains.

'Then you *are* a gentleman,' she says, 'and, no doubt, an educated one.'

'I am just an apprentice,' he continues. 'I survive on a meagre stipend and the unpredictable charity of my employer.'

'Ah!' she says, offering a smile. 'But when your apprenticeship is concluded you'll have chambers at Lincoln's Inn and grow rich from the gratitude of duchesses and dowager widows whose estates you'll defend.'

'Perhaps.'

'I feel sure of it.'

He seems to relax a little in her company and throws her a sidelong smile. 'I like your flower,' he offers, nodding at the gerbera daisy tucked into the hatband of her straw boater.

'It's my name, sir,' she says.

'Your name?'

'Daisy.'

'Oh,' he says. 'A pretty name indeed. And a very pretty trademark.'

She slants an eye in his direction.

'For a very pretty lady,' he adds.

She smiles at the compliment. 'There's a costermonger at Spitalfields market who's taken a shine to me. Each day he offers me a fresh bloom, and a new song.'

'I am not surprised,' he replies. 'But, if you'll pardon my enquiry in return, you're not from London, are you Daisy?' He has detected the roundness in her accent, the fullness and curve of intonation that somehow seems to complement her figure.

'I'm from the Westcountry, sir, from the Bill at Portland to be precise.'

'Really?' A frown settles on his expression. 'But why exchange such a wonderful part of the world for this?' He stops to gesture at the pall of fog on every side.

'To follow my dream, sir,' she says.

'And what might that be?' he asks.

'To be an actress.'

'Oh.' He seems unsure how to proceed. They walk together in silence until he gives his intrigue voice. 'And how does that go?'

She grins. 'Very well indeed, sir.'

'Truly?' He turns to her.

'Most truly.'

'Then where do you play?'

'Nearby, at the Nightingale, just off Whitechapel Road. Do you know it?'

'Well, yes. I am no patron of the arts, but I have heard of it.' His eyes narrow. 'But I am told the Nightingale only offers performances of *phantasmagoria* – magic lantern shows of devils, spectres and skeletons, projected onto smoke and accompanied by screams, cymbal clashes and ghastly melodies played on the glass harmonium. Such performances are spectacles only and require no skilled actors to give them life.'

Her fingers dance along his sleeve. 'Then you are misinformed,' she says. 'You may find *phantasmagoria* at the Apollinaire, or the Lyceum on the Strand, but not the Nightingale.' She inclines her head a little in confession. 'Although, you are *partly* right – the Nightingale's shows are also in the style of *Théâtre Optique*.'

'An illusion?'

'But only to the untrained eye.'

'I do not follow.'

'Our performances are presented as illusion, yet they are in fact, very real.'

'Why such complexity? What purpose does this deception serve?'

She gathers her thoughts to explain. 'Tell me, if you went to watch *phantasmagoria*, would you perceive it as truth or illusion?'

'Illusion.'

'Plainly?'

'Most plainly. Childish tricks of the light will not fool me.'

'Is this not also because, when you attend a performance of *phantasmagoria*, it is *illusion* you expect to see?'

'I suppose.'

'Then what if you came to the Nightingale in a similar frame of mind, expecting only some crude, optical trickery. Yet what you encounter is a spectacle so real, so lifelike, that you would question your judgement. Would this not be more confounding, more amazing than the simple trick of *phantasmagoria*? Would this not represent the greater attraction?'

'Then yes, it would.' He gives a small laugh. 'And I suppose it is the Nightingale's cast of actors – actors like yourself – that gives this false illusion such heightened credibility?'

She smiles.

'Ingenious,' he offers. 'Most ingenious.'

'But what I tell you is a secret,' she says. 'A *stage secret.*'

'I understand,' he says.

'You should read our reviews in the broadsheets.'

'Perhaps I should.'

'You should come.'

'Perhaps I will.'

'We play to a full house every night.'

He nods, considering, as they walk to the end of the street and stop. He lifts his cane. 'The Nightingale is this way?'

'It is.'

He lifts his cane in the other direction. 'My lodging lies this way.' He bows a little and thumbs the brim of his hat. 'Good-night to you Daisy.' He seems reluctant to leave, as if he might lose her in the fog forever.

Her smile is warm and fragile. 'You do not need money,' she says.

He shakes his head, not understanding.

She grasps his collar and pulls his hatstand frame down to her own height. Then, leaning close, she breathes into his ear. 'There are other ways to repay a lady for her favour.' She lifts a knee along the inside of his thigh. He lets out a long breath that parts the fog. 'See me safely to the Nightingale and I'll show you, if you like.'

'Very well.' His whisper is cracked.

Once again she takes his arm and guides him. The cold air in the unlit street hangs dense and damp. Darkness circles them like a prowling beast. He taps his cane from side to side, to keep them in the middle way and safe from anything that may block their path.

'One day they'll light these damnable streets with gas lamps,' he offers in reassurance. 'Like other parts of the city.'

She knows this to be true. Many of the well-heeled of London now walk in safety at night. But the lamplit streets of Grosvenor Square and St. James's Park are three omnibus fares and half a world away. And this is Spitalfields.

'Perhaps you might care to tell me now?' he ventures.

She cannot see his face but hears the nervous entreaty in his voice. 'Tell you what?'

His voice falls close to soundlessness. 'How best I might earn your favour.'

'Just a simple favour in return.'

'But can you not explain it?'

'I can, but it's easier to show you,' she says.

In the distance, a glow suffuses the haze and makes clear a row of squat houses glistening in the dampness. The shadows of people, distorted and giant-like, play across the wet brickwork. Closer, and they can hear voices: a low murmur of conversation deadened by the fog. The thin sound of a ballad played upon a penny whistle reaches them. Together, they walk towards the light and sound, more quickly and more surely than before. She leads him around a corner and they stop. The coloured oil lamps of the Nightingale Theatre pierce the cloaked night. A long line of theatre-goers waits patiently outside the entrance and upon its steps. They talk, stamp their feet, and blow into cupped hands. He lifts his arm free from hers and walks towards the light of the theatre, gazing at the garish posters pasted onto Doric columns. She tuts and pulls him away by the elbow, into a darkened side-street and up a flight of stone steps. At the very top she produces an iron key, unlocks the door, and beckons him inside.

◂—●—▸

'My employer, and proprietor of the Nightingale Theatre,' she announces with a hand extended in my direction and something of the illusionist's assistant in her manner. I turn from my desk in the dusty backstage prop-room that now serves as my studio. In her eyes I see her triumph and, when I see *him*, I understand why.

I leap to my feet and rush forward. He offers both a hand in greeting and look of alarm, as if he were a man about to be attacked but determined to accept it with uncommon courtesy. Ignoring the proffered hand, I grasp his chin and turn his face to left and right. He stammers an incomplete greeting through clenched teeth. His profile is a sensation.

'Most suitable,' I mumble. I slap his shoulders and step back to admire the entirety of him. I walk around him, examining every detail: the perfection of his narrow limbs, the rounded, stooping shoulders, the forward cant of a neck too slender for its shirt-collar, the lean fingers tapering from bony knuckles, the rangy, lanky, gangling length and height of the man. He is a stick-figure, a child's drawing, a tailor's nightmare. And that nose. That chin.

I am a whirlwind of industry now. I hurry about the studio collecting all the apparatus I need. With a hook-pole I pull down the phosphorous-coated screen and unwrap its lower section across the floorboards. Upon this, and at its very centre, I place a simple wooden chair, patting its seat in gesture of invitation.

'Sit there,' she directs him.

'But what is happening?' he asks. His voice is shrill.

'This is the simple favour I ask of you.'

I assemble the tripods and mount the polished copper dish of the *Geistag Illuminator*. Then I fill its lamp-tray with fresh flash powder. She leads him to the chair. Bewildered, he sits.

'But what in the Devil's name *is* this?' he asks.

She stands behind him and places soothing hands on his shoulders and neck. 'There is no need for concern. It will only take a minute.' She bends low. Her voice is faint. 'Then we can be together.'

'She is correct,' I say, attempting to calm him. I place the camera upon its tripod. 'It's just a simple image technique.'

'A *daguerreotype*?' he asks the room in general, then, to her: 'Why did you not tell me?'

'Not a daguerreotype,' I explain. 'More of a *photogram*.' I paint a single glass plate with wet collodion, then place another plate of glass over it. 'It is my own process, I call it a *shadowgraph*.' Carefully, I place the glass plates inside the camera.

'You mean to take my image?' he asks.

'Your *shadow*,' I correct him.

'A silhouette?' he says.

'Of sorts,' I say.

'For me,' she adds.

He looks up at her. 'For you?'

'To remember you by.' She smiles a boudoir smile at him.

'But, but…' he attempts to rise but she eases him back with gentle hands upon his shoulders. 'You mean to take my image without my permission?'

'We do not have your permission?' I ask with practised incredulity. 'Then why are you here?'

'Do it for me,' her soft voice urges him. 'And I'll return the favour.'

His mouth gapes wide, no words come, and so I take my chance. I cross to the fireplace and light a long taper. I lift my chin at her and she follows my signal, moving away from him and covering her eyes with a forearm. I recross the room. 'Don't move,' I command him, then I uncap the lens and light the flash powder.

The room becomes the centre of the sun.

He screams. Then leaps to his feet.

'I said do not move!'

'I cannot see!'

'The blindness is only temporary,' I explain. She goes to him now, and takes him by the arm in comfort. On the phosphorous screen his shadow burns. I only need to keep the lens clear now – to let the camera do its work.

I count the long seconds while the shadow fades, then I replace the cap and it is done.

He pushes her roughly away now. 'I don't know who you are, or what you want...' He stumbles about the room – a blind, angry man. 'This is *most* irregular,' he shouts. He appears to make sense of his surroundings. His vision is returning. He sees the door that led him in. He strides towards it, his long legs striking table ends and chair legs in the path of his escape. 'Irregular, irregular,' he repeats. '*Most* irregular!' He half-strides, half-falls through the doorway and down the stairs to the street. As his sight returns he will come to know what he has left behind, what he has lost. He will realise that he no longer walks with a shadow.

———— ◂ • ▸ ————

The fog hides things.

It hides the soot on window ledges and renders the colours of damp laundry on washing lines to flags of dullest grey.

It hides the squalor, the rubbish and rat-runs.

It hides the deeds of the desperate and dishonest.

It hides the dead of the impoverished.

It hides the violence of men and the blood of women.

Most of all it hides our shadows: the very proof of our being, of our humanity.

For in the fog, no living thing may cast a shadow.

Our shadows are the darker half of our souls. We are creatures of light and darkness. We are binary, conjoined: night and day, sun and moon, knowledge and faith, male and female, good and evil. Without one, the other simply does not exist.

This is the balance of shadow and light. The balance of the universe.

But in the fog there are no shadows.

So the shadowless wraiths who live a half-life dwell here, unnoticed and undetected. These are the unwhole, the unholy. These are the *unshadowed* – and the fog hides them well. He is one of them now, and only in the fog will he be at home. Only in the fog will he find peace.

———◆———

The auditorium of the Nightingale is filled with chatter and a sense of expectation. Every seat is filled and the house lamps reveal the simplicity of the arrangement. Nothing is hidden, everything is open to inspection. This is the greatest part of the spectacle, its lack of trickery, its naked, laid-bare honesty. In the midst of the audience, on a trestle table, stand the three magic lanterns I will operate. Upon the stage, the curtains are drawn back to reveal only the whitewashed bricks of the stage wall. There is no other artifice.

From a wheeled, *secretaire* steamer trunk, I remove the first of the glass plates and place it in a lantern. The house lights are snuffed and she sits beside me while the theatre becomes dark. I light the lantern. The audience falls to silence, then emits a long gasp of wonder as the shadow appears. The white bricks at the back of the stage are washed with luminescence. In the middle of this glowing space, a dark blur forms. It solidifies, and takes shape as a man sitting on a chair. A murmur of appreciation goes round, followed by a wave of applause. The shadow of the man seems to hear it and looks up. He stands now, slowly. He is tall and thin, a hatstand of a man with a pick-axe nose and a pointed chin that rises to meet it. Someone laughs and the shadow looks in the direction from which the laughter came. More laughter. The hatstand man looks about, as if he has just awoken in a bedchamber he does not know. He walks from left to right, assessing his place of confinement. He is all knees and elbows, striding around with an ungainly, loose-limbed gait. The audience laughs loudly. The shadow reacts with terror, then places both hands upon his head as if uttering a silent scream.

Ever since I paid my first visit to *Le Chat Noir*, that great *Théâtre d'Ombres* in Montmartre, have I been obsessed with the shadow-play. The paring-back of its imagery to simple form, shape and shadow creates space enough for the mind to extemporise and provide the details it does not see. The effect is most illusory, yet complete; magical, yet real. I have striven for a lifetime to create my own version of it, something more miraculous, more astonishing – something that will cause the mind to distrust the eyes, and our faculties to confound our reason. I began with back-projections and simple paper puppets in the style of the *Indochine* masters. In my quest for realism I advanced to jointed zinc figures then, dispirited by the harshness of their outlines I clothed them in soft, gauzy fabrics, crowned their heads with human hair and adorned each setting with filigreed props and lacework. My next approach took a more scientific direction: with lenses and more powerful oxyhydrogen lamps I created layers of varied focus in an attempt to mimic that depth of dimension as perceived by the human eye. Try as I might, nothing approximated the natural, living beauty of the images that haunted me. Only in my unrelated experiments with photograms did I discover, quite by accident, the correct chemistry to make my ambition reality. With the gift of this strange alchemy I saw the possibilities of its application, and a wonderful new conjuring of this most experiential of theatrical arts.

From the *secretaire* trunk, I remove a second plate of glass, slide it into another of the lanterns and light the wick. The stage wall glows brighter and a second shadow appears. It blooms from its tiny, blurred centre, into the silhouette of a woman. As one, the audience roars with approval. Some are on their feet, others applaud wildly. They know her. She stands, hands on hips, at one side of the stage, watching the hatstand man pace hither and thither. She has an hourglass figure with a tiny waist and wears a straw boater with a single flower tucked inside its hatband.

The shadow of the man appears to see her and halts. There is another round of applause at this face-off between shadows. The members of the audience nearest me turn and cast inquisitive eyes over the lanterns. I sit back and let the shadows play while they search for the trickery in the spectacle. They find none, and their wonder is complete. They will spread word of this, and the queue outside the Nightingale will grow nightly.

The shadow of the hourglass woman walks towards the hatstand man, her hips tilt in coquettish suggestion. He steps back and she slips her shawl to her waist in display of herself, then faces the audience. A cheer goes up. At this, the hatstand man recoils and run in circles until he collides with the chair, entangling its legs in his own.

The laughter is deafening. Men rap their canes against the floorboards. Some are doubled in mirth or slap their thighs, their faces streaked with tears.

She is so unlike the others. I see them here from time to time. Their memory whispers to them that this is the place of their unshadowing and so they come to sit in silent sorrow in the rowdy, rollicking aisles and search the images on the wall for the lost part of themselves. I do not know what happens to them after that. Perhaps they give themselves to misery, or pine away.

I turn to watch her. Her face is aglow in the lantern light. She smiles. It is the smile she reserves for me and for this occasion: a smile without theatrics, unscripted and unrehearsed. A smile as broad as a Portland sky.

Tomorrow I know she will ask me the same question: when will her job be finished? When will I reunite her with her darker self? I will tell her that I work hard towards a solution, that one day I will make her whole again. But I know this is a lie. I know that once severed, darkness and light can never be rejoined. This suits my selfishness, for I can never part with her. She is the greatest actress I know. She is the original, the first I ever captured.

Yet now I know the truth: it was she who captured me.

For now, she is content.

She is content to sweep her attic room, content to gaze from her oriel window towards domes and spires she cannot see.

She is content to work alongside me in the theatre, to help with the expanding of my collection.

By day she is content to move, undetected, among the living and the whole – my thief of shadows, my huntress in the fog.

But it is here, at night, that she is most content. Content to see herself as she has always dreamed.

Immortalised, and loved by all, upon a London stage.

7

LAZLO THE UNFORMED

SHE'S DONE IT AGAIN.

Once more my sister has led me astray.

She's dragged me away from something I'd set my heart on, towards some shiny new object that's caught her eye. As usual it's ended badly.

I stand on the South Parade Pier outside the Pavilion of Peculiarities, betrayed and sixpenceless.

All I'd wanted was a toffee apple.

'Give me back my money!' she shouts at a boy of around my own age. He stands near the Pavilion's entrance beside a makeshift ticket counter, head tilted backwards as if avoiding physical attack. From his neck to his knees he's clothed in a loose, tan-coloured smock. It looks out of place, more suited to a struggling artist in his garret or a Dorset potato farmer in his meadow.

'Now!' my sister screams.

The boy's eyes grow wide and for the first time I notice how spectacular they are: one eye glitters green as an emerald, the other sparkles blue as a cut sapphire.

My sister advances on him, palm thrust out. 'My *shilling*. I gave it to the old man here before.'

The boy's brilliant eyes narrow. 'To be *pree-cise*, it was two sixpenny pieces,' he says.

It's strange how he knows this but he's right. We had paid for our tickets of admission to the Pavilion with two sixpences. Mine, and my sister's. A tall, gaunt gentleman with a bent spine received our coins into knotty hands. He'd worn a similar cassock and it now occurs to me this must be the adoptive uniform of sideshow workers and carnival folk in general. As well as painters and potato farmers.

Papa had pressed the silver coins into our palms only a short time before. 'Why don't you two treat yourselves to something on the pier?' he'd said. Then he loosened his tie, unbuttoned his collar and slumped into one of the striped canvas deckchairs he'd dragged onto the shingle beach for Mama and himself. Mama shot us a brief smile of encouragement then immured herself in a copy of *Harper's*. Papa tipped his trilby over his eyes. *Leave us alone* was the very clear message.

I looked at the sixpence in my hand and knew what I'd do.

I would try my arm at the hoop-la or perhaps the coconut shy, making sure I left pennies enough for a toffee apple. In my imagination I saw the hoops land with deadly accuracy over bags of goldfish, cap-guns and clockwork cars of pressed metal. At the coconut shy the wooden ball would leave my hand in a dangerous arc, dislodging coconut after coconut. Then, struggling with my trophies, I'd taste the fracture of caramel glazing between my teeth and the sweet white fruit inside. It was the perfect plan.

Yet I hadn't planned on my sister robbing me for her own ends. She'd pinched, pummelled and pestered the sixpence out of my grasp for a visit to the Pavilion of Peculiarities.

And here we are.

The boy's bicoloured eyes are defensive. 'On what grounds?' he asks.

'We are dissatisfied,' my sister announces as if suddenly becoming a member of the royal family.

'How so?' The boy raises an eyebrow. A most feminine eyebrow I now observe. His lashes are long.

My sister turns to gesture at the painted canvas hanging across the entrance to the Pavilion. It's bright with images of the attractions inside. Written in bold, showground lettering are promises of fascination, fear and delight. She seems speechless with anger and can only point and flail her arm at the canvas in attempt of explanation.

My attention is pulled away, from my sister, from the Pavilion and the gaudy, playbill artwork. I'm drawn to something that drifts on the air like temptation. Something I know but cannot name. It floats amidst briny smells of rotting kelp that drift up from below the pier. It's infused with all the fairground odours of frying onions, vinegar from the cockle stalls, axle grease, chip fat and paraffin.

I breathe in, separating this pot pourri into its separate aromas. Then I find it – *burnt sugar* – and the tangy, orchard-ripe bouquet of apples.

My eyes find its source. The carousel and Ferris wheel slow, their colours dim. Sounds of laughter and music from the fair organs are hushed. In the centre of the pier is a stall, gaily lit, within it a tiered display where row upon row of upended toffee apples point their sticks toward the summer sky. They shine, bright green and blood red, encased in caramel as thick as glass.

My mouth waters. I sigh.

'It's a sham!' my sister shrieks. 'All of it!'

I'm drawn back to the confrontation at the Pavilion. My sister has found her voice again. 'Nothing in here is real!' She levels a finger at the boy and announces for the benefit of all those within earshot: 'You're a fraud!'

Heads turn in our direction. Brows lower. The boy at the entrance to the Pavilion shifts from foot to foot but beams with good nature. He offers a defence to the passing crowd, as much as to my sister. 'Now, now, miss. Everything inside the Pavilion of Peculiarities is one hundred percent genuine, guaranteed.' His voice is reedy, higher. It matches my sister's in tone and pitch.

'Guaranteed, huh?'

The boy nods. Perhaps my preoccupation with the toffee apples has caused me not to notice before but his face is pretty for a boy, his lips rosebud-like.

'And who makes this *guarantee*?' my sister presses.

'We do.'

'And who is "we"?'

The boy blinks for an instant then places delicate hands over his heart. 'We are,' he offers.

My sister's eyelids flutter in confusion. She wheels around to march up and down in front of the draped canvas. She stops and points. 'Well, what about this? How can you guarantee *this* is real?'

The boy cranes forward displaying a slender neck. His eyes follow my sister's finger to one of the attractions displayed on the canvas. 'Ah yes.' He smiles. 'The Two-Headed Horse of Sturminster. A rare marvel indeed, and completely genuine...'

'But it's dead,' my sister observes, unimpressed.

'Quite dead, yes,' agrees the boy.

'It probably never lived.'

'Perhaps so. It would be difficult for a two-headed horse to make its way in the world...'

'It's just an – *embryo*,' says my sister, 'floating in a tank of pickling vinegar.'

'*Formaldehyde*, to be *pree-cise*.'

She stamps a foot causing her ringlets to dance and points at the canvas again. 'Then why is it portrayed here as a fully grown chestnut mare in bridle and harness ridden by a man in a top hat?'

The boy waves a hand in dismissal. 'But this is just an *advertisement* – a way to excite the imagination, nothing more.'

'But it's a *lie*.'

The boy tilts his head to left and right, considering. 'We find that people are generally accepting of a little creative licence. No one ever takes these kinds of things literally.' The colourful eyes narrow, holding a question. He nods to the image on the canvas. 'Tell me, did you really believe this is what you'd find inside?'

Her voice is small, uncertain. 'Yes.'

His delicate eyebrow arches. 'Then really – *who* has deceived *whom*?'

Whom? It strikes me that he doesn't speak like a boy. I'd never use such a word. I wouldn't know how.

My sister and the boy lock eyes. His sparkle blue and green. Hers burn a fierce blue like the flame of our gas stove. She pieces her indignation back together, wheels towards the canvas and points once more. 'Then what about this – the Genie's Dungeon?' Beneath her finger lies the image of a demon bound by chains. His hair is all fire, his skin black scales. His lips wear a lascivious grin.

The boy straightens, his voice solemn. 'The Prison of Shudesh the Vile.'

'It's not like this picture. Not one bit.'

'Ah, but it *is*...'

'It's just a bottle. A perfume bottle.'

'A *djinn* bottle, to be *pree-cise*.'

'A gin bottle?'

'Quite so. It was crafted by the priests of Baalbek to imprison Shudesh for his countless crimes against mankind.'

'But it's empty.'

The boy's laugh is high, bell-like. 'Well, it might appear that way. It's because the glass is clear and Shudesh is a formless spirit...'

'It's empty,' repeats my sister. 'The bottle is open, the top's removed.'

The boy gasps. He looks at me. 'Is this true?'

I nod. We'd found the bottle of lumpy, weathered glass lying on a pedestal on its side. Sealing wax from the top had been picked away. The stopper was pulled from the bottle and now lay beside it.

The boy's hands fly to his face. Long fingernails cover his eyes but fail to hide his alarm. He searches both ends of the pier with a feverish gaze. 'This won't do, this won't do at all,' he murmurs. Until now I had thought his hair to be clipped short. Now I see that it's long and tucked up into a tight bun at the back of his head.

'Oh, you are *good*,' my sister gloats.

His attention snaps back to her. 'Good?'

'A good actor.' She crosses her arms.

His look is wounded. 'I assure you this is no *act*. It's a catastrophe!'

I now begin to question whether he is a boy at all. His look, voice and bearing have become so androgynous.

My sister continues her offensive, in full pursuit of our two sixpenny pieces. Turning, she selects another image from the canvas. 'And just how real is this – *the Eye of the Gorgon*?' On the canvas is the painted head of a woman with glowing eyes, her head a crown of serpents.

The boy – *or girl* – at the ticket counter is lost to the present. He, or she, mutters to themself, scanning the length and breadth of the pier with frantic apprehension.

'*This*!' shouts my sister, finger thrust at the image on the canvas. 'It's not *real*, is it?'

Her insistence brings the boy back from whatever cataclysm he's been imagining. 'That's *Algol*,' he explains. 'It carries the same name as that unlucky star in the constellation of Perseus. It's rumoured to be the eye of the terrible Medusa herself...'

'Truly?'

'Most truly...'

'It's a rock,' says my sister without emotion.

The boy – or girl, I still don't know which – raises a wiry eyebrow white as hoarfrost. 'A *fossil*, to be *pree-cise*,' he or she says.

'How convenient. I could say the same of any harmless stone found on the beach.'

'Algol is not harmless. The eye is *real* – and most deadly,' the boy or girl insists. 'That's why the exhibit is roped off and the eye placed in a sealed glass case facing a mirror. To look at it directly is to invite certain death.'

My sister's smile is rueful. 'Which explains all the props – to make us think it's real?'

'What props?'

'The statues.'

'What statues?' Both eyebrows are raised now. Both are wiry, white.

'The statues that stand *inside* the roped-off area. Behind the case. They gaze at the eye without the benefit of the mirror,' my sister explains.

They'd been so lifelike, the statues behind the Gorgon's Eye. They held me with a kind of grim fascination. It was like standing before figures in a waxworks that might spring to life at any second. The idea that a head might turn in my direction caused a slow, trembling coldness to move over me. I was amazed that such softness, the weave and creases of cloth, the gentle folds of skin and strands of hair, could be reproduced so truthfully into the hardness of rock. Whoever had crafted such realistic figures was an artist beyond parallel. A young man and woman, fixed in stone, stood behind the cabinet, bent towards the eye itself. I could make out the finest details: the smoothness of the woman's cheeks, the fur of her stole, the man's watch chain, the rings on his fingers, and their shared, wide-eyed expression of terror.

A tear wells in the eye of the boy who might be a girl, then slides chinward. 'No. This must not be...'

To me his grief seems genuine but my sister taps silent

fingertips together in mock applause. Her smile grows broad. 'Bravo,' she squeals.

Girlboy's head droops. The hair is streaked with grey and I wonder whether these events have aged him. Or her. 'I'll have to engage a stonemason with mallet and chisel, before they are recognised. I'll scatter them on the beach like pebbles, or cast them into the sea.' He sobs now.

My sister presses her advantage. 'Thanks for the performance. Now, return our shilling.'

Girlboy looks up. The white eyebrows knit. 'Why? Everything you have seen is real.'

'Is it?' Her eyes flare, gas-stove blue. 'Is it – *really*?'

'Why, yes.' Girlboy tugs at an ear. I watch the lobe stretch, long and pliable, like plasticine. The ear slides and elongates, becomes leathery and wrinkled. I feel myself catch breath. My sister seems not to notice and instead directs her rage to the painted canvas once more.

'Then how real is *this*?' she protests. 'We never even saw it! What, or *who* is *Lazlo the Unformed*?'

The painting on the canvas is complex, unclear. It's a face – this much I can see, yet one side of the face appears to be female while the other is male. Each half is further divided into what seems to be representations of youth and old age. The image is a muddle of grey whiskers and bright eyes, masculine features, feminine beauty and crumbling frailty.

'I am Lazlo.'

We turn back. Girlboy's face is older now, etched with lines.

My sister points at the painted face on the canvas.

'This is supposed to be you?' She huffs with derision.

Lazlo draws a long breath and nods. In the fabric of the tan-coloured smock I see movement. A breast grows, rounds into fullness, then droops, pendulous with age.

'In what way are you *unformed*?' demands my sister, oblivious.

'All the usual ways,' offers Lazlo.

My sister shakes her head with scorn. 'Nonsense.'

Lazlo reaches into a pocket and produces two silver coins. 'Then here is your money.'

Quick as a viper my sister snatches a coin away. Retreating, she offers a sidelong look. 'Why?' she asks.

Lazlo studies the remaining sixpence between finger and thumb. His words are hung with sadness. 'Because this is all you believe in. There is no wonder in you.' Then Lazlo offers the last bright coin to me.

The fairground smells pull at me again like temptation. Burnt sugar and sweet fruit linger and drift. I turn in the direction of the toffee apple stall. Under glassy, shining caramel the bottle-green and ruby-red apples gleam like navigation lamps, guiding me in. The Ferris wheel and carousel slow. Laughter and music are hushed. Lights dim. I could walk there now. I could grasp one of the top-heavy fruits by its stick. I could lift it to my mouth. I could close my eyes and delight in that first splintering bite.

But I don't.

I turn back and fold the remaining coin into Lazlo's wrinkling palm.

I hear my sister's gasp of shock. Then I feel her hand on my collar, dragging me away.

As I trip and stumble over the pier's uneven floorboards, I steal one last look at the Pavilion of Peculiarities.

An old woman stands near the makeshift ticket counter, in front of the brightly painted canvases. Her back is bowed, her white hair is raked into a tight bun. From her neck to her knees she is clothed in a loose, tan-coloured smock. Between finger and thumb she holds a shining coin.

Then she lifts her head to me and winks.

One eye blue. The other green.

8

THE FOREVER CHILD

THE BABE SHIFTS inside you.

With your fingernail you tap a tooth as the question forms.

Why had you not thought to ask it before?

You – who gazed upon the towers of Byzantium.

You – who stepped unnoticed down the centuries and drank the wisdom of the world.

Why only now do you ask?

You never thought to ask it on that warm, bright night when you arched a brow in his direction and speared him with a promise. Or as you led him from the laughing crowd, along quiet streets and up your dark stairs.

You never thought to ask it as you undressed him, as your bodies joined in desire's timeless alchemy and creation set to work inside you. Or afterwards even, when you feasted on him.

Only now do you ask this...

What will my child be like?

You sense the truth as the crowning of its head begins to tear you open. As you scream into the linings of your casket.

This child will be like you: immortal.

It will never age. Toothless, it will never feed but only mewl and cling to you.

It shall forever fix you with black eyes and suckle on the blood that swells your breast.

You will always love this child, but the lamps you thought would light your way to joy are all snuffed out.

Children are a blessing, yes.

But blessings can be curses, too.

9

THE HIDDEN

TOBY HIGGINS was hiding again.

This time he was hiding from *cabbage*.

He justified the act as an important one. It wasn't all about *him*. He was hiding on behalf of all children like himself who detested the slimy, colourless slop they pushed to the farthest edges of their plates. Cabbage offered nothing in terms of aesthetic or nutrition. Any goodness it contained was boiled away. It didn't even taste of anything. It was an excuse for a vegetable, something to make up the numbers in the obligatory *meat-and-two-veg*. A stopgap. An afterthought. Cabbage was irrelevant, a meaningless institution. As such, it had to be opposed, struggled against, overthrown.

He told himself he was hiding for the greater good.

He was hiding for *a cause*.

Toby craned upwards, surveying the interior of the tall linen cupboard. The top shelf should do it. He climbed the shelves like the rungs of a ladder and slipped inside, wrapping himself in the warmth of flannelette sheets and cotton pillowcases. Then he reached out and pulled the door closed by the coat hook fixed to the inside.

For now there was silence. Soon his mother would call him to the dinner table, her frustration mounting in a shrill crescendo. Then his father would shout. Exhortations at first, then demands, then threats. He'd hear his mother's shoes ring against the passage floorboards and thump up the stairs to the bedroom landing. She'd check the locks and windows. His father would check the coal bunker and the cupboard under the staircase. The small terrace house would be filled with the sounds of upheaval. Dinner would cool upon the table forcing them to call off their search. His mother would lament while his father would saw a little too physically at his cutlet. There would be talk of boarding schools and cadet college, home tutors, strict governesses and other disciplinary measures. Toby would doze in the warmth. He'd face the consequences tomorrow. For now he was comfortable and as far away from cabbage as he could get. He'd sleep deeply, then wake in the middle of the night and crawl back to his own bed. By morning the fire of his parents' anger would have burnt itself out. His mother would be relieved he was safe. His father would promise to deal with him later, then hurry off to work.

Toby was a master of concealment. He was small for his age and unusually flexible which meant he could bend himself into odd shapes and not feel discomfort for hours on end. He could curl into the majority of his mother's hatboxes, her valise, and his father's Gladstone bag. He could hang from coat hooks, obscured among overcoats and Mackintoshes. He could even hide in the empty bottom drawer of the Welsh dresser and manage to pull it closed once inside. On one occasion he squeezed himself into the movement of the grandfather clock. His timing had been poor, however, and the clock struck the hour with a muffled peal like a bell in a blanket, or the sound the piano made when Toby bumped into it.

His mother believed that if hiding was ever recognised as a legitimate sport, then the shelves in Toby's room would groan with trophies. His father believed that Toby's skills would qualify him for a career in espionage and that he should contact the Foreign Office at the earliest conclusion of his studies. Toby delighted in the idea that he might one day earn money for doing what he did best. He resolved to become a spy and could think of no nobler calling than hiding for his country. He even wrote a letter to the Prime Minister offering his services but received no reply.

It wasn't just cabbage that Toby hid from.

He hid from school gymnastics, cricket practice and cross-country runs. He hid from most forms of physical exercise and any instruction in studies he deemed outdated or impractical. He hid from Latin lessons and studies of the classics in general. He hid from homework, he hid from chores. He hid from parlour games and any kind of imposed entertainment like trips to the seaside or rambles in the country. He hid from church services, visits to the dentist and the barber. He hid from the larger boys at school and the more boisterous girls. He hid from anyone who was bigger, noisier, smarter, or more popular. It was generally agreed that Toby hid from himself as much as he hid from the world around him.

One afternoon during the week while Toby was at large in the family home, his mother called for him. He found her seated at the roll-top desk in the drawing room with an opened letter in her hand.

She wore a pair of wire-rimmed reading spectacles and a look of incredulity.

'You've been invited to a party,' she announced with disbelief.

Toby began to palpitate. His gaze darted to left and right, to the sanctuary of shadow behind the opened door, the corner of the room between the bookcase and the curtains, the darkness beneath the fringed valance of the winged armchair.

'A birthday party for Lorelei Blake,' his mother continued. 'I never even knew the Blakes had a daughter – did you?'

Toby stopped breathing. The universe compressed into a tiny, dense molecule, then exploded in a shower of sparks.

Lorelei.

'Did you Toby? Did you know the Blakes had a daughter?' his mother went on.

It was easy to overlook Lorelei. Especially in the presence of her parents. Her father was a huge, gouty man with a heavy footfall. Her mother was spherical and overly ornamented. Her parents weren't just large, they were *planetary*. They rumbled around with little regard for their surroundings, taking up far more space than they deserved. Locked in their gravity was Lorelei, orbiting around them, in and out of their shadow, a tiny, celestial object, bright and elusive. Toby had first seen her with her parents in the confectioner's on the High Street. He'd watched her through the glass of a half-empty liquorice jar while she nibbled on a penny swirl almost as big as her face. Her skin was pale as a newly risen moon, her eyes dark as secrecy. She'd looked in his direction, then she'd smiled. It takes a hider to know a hider.

Of course the Blakes had a daughter.

And Toby had adored her from the first.

'Toby, are you listening to me?' His mother's voice seemed to tug him by the ear, back to the drawing room with the roll-top desk. She waved the letter at him with a smile that didn't suit her. It was girlish, rueful. 'And I think you're going to like this…' She re-positioned her reading glasses on her nose and read from the letter. 'Lorelei will celebrate her birthday with an afternoon of *hide and seek*.'

Toby gasped. The muse of the clandestine arts had smiled upon him. By these means, Lorelei had given him the opportunity to both prove his worth and win her heart. It was perfect. It would be his great victory, his *magnum opus*. He'd hide like he'd never hidden before. One moment he'd be there, the next – gone. He'd vanish like smoke, quickly as a new year's resolution. After the party the other children would question whether he'd been there at all. What was he – a shadow, a spectre? Toby imagined himself winning round after round of the game, defeating all Lorelei's suitors. If this was to be a tournament in her honour, then Toby would be her champion.

The weeks ground slowly by. Toby lost sleep, he grew thinner than normal. He knew nothing of the layout of the Blakes' residence and this consumed him. He knew the house was large but, unlike all the familiar hidey-holes of the Higgins' small terrace, he had no idea of the challenge he'd be faced with. He'd have to be fast, resourceful.

The Saturday of the party found him walking the half-mile out of town to Lorelei's house. He wore his Sunday best (which had seen very little use) and carried a birthday card in an envelope. He'd agonised for days over the inscription. He didn't want to gush, neither did he wish to appear cold or aloof.

The episode had been as painful as toothache.

He stood at last, gazing through the railings of Blake Hall. The house was more vast than he could ever have imagined. At its centre was a once-modest manor in the Queen Anne style with pink bricks and a portico of white columns topped with a triangular pediment. From this humble beginning sprawled the later additions: the extra wings and façades of varying architectural influence – the halls, domes, colonnades and galleries. The place seemed to have grown beyond all proportion, much like the Blakes themselves. The house presided over an estate of at least eighty acres with tracts of woodland and a flat expanse of reed-fringed mere.

Toby's head spun. He calculated there would be thousands, if not millions of places to hide in a house like this. He'd have to resist indecision. He'd need to stay focussed for his plan to succeed.

He announced himself at the vestibule and was ushered into the main hall. Here a collection of rowdy children was already at play. Lorelei sat alone, beside a table laden with presents wrapped in brightly coloured paper. Toby felt instantly inadequate. He held out the envelope in offering and approached with grave ceremony. Lorelei took it.

'Aren't you going to wish me a happy birthday, Toby?' Her words were soft.

'Ah, yes, why yes I am,' he stammered. He felt his cheeks burn.

She cocked an eyebrow at him.

'And here it is, my, ah, my birthday wish for you...'

A smile hid behind Lorelei's eyes.

'I, ah, I wish for you – a most happy birthday dear Lorelei.' Then, to his own surprise, he held a hand to his chest and bowed.

When he looked up her smile had revealed itself. And it was glorious.

Lorelei's mother appeared, crashing through the proceedings like a meteorite. She set about organising everyone in a loud voice that rattled the china tea set. As host, Lorelei was the first to seek. She began her count to one hundred as the other children dispersed. Toby took his time, he walked an opposite direction to every other hider he encountered. While they opted for the amateur locations in wardrobes and beneath beds, he headed deeper into the house, looking for the dark places, the places only he in his inestimable skill could appreciate and take advantage of.

His instincts led him downstairs into the kitchens. The rooms were unlit and the serving staff absent, perhaps they'd been given the afternoon off. Toby crawled into the huge oven and curled inside a roasting pan. He thought to steal an apple from the larder and place it in his mouth for comic effect but realised the idea was pointless. He wouldn't be found and no one would see it.

One by one the hiders were discovered and his name was called as winner. He emerged and walked back to the great hall, taking careful note of potential hiding places along the way. He stopped at the darkened doorway of the scullery. Something urged him to step inside, to inspect it more closely. In the dim light he found little of interest save a hatch in the wall. He slid the hatch upwards and drew a long breath.

It was a dumb waiter. A small, hand-operated lift that ferried hot food from the kitchens to the servery beside the dining room on the floor above. The interior was black as pitch so he felt inside, making out the shape of a simple box of panelled wood, open on the hatch side. Two ropes hung within. One pulled the counterweighted box upwards, the other pulled it down.

Toby drew the hatch back into place and schemed. This was good. He'd save this for last – for his grand finale, his *coup de grâce*.

Room by room and game after game, Toby learned more about the house. His hiding places became more ingenious, more obscure. Each time he was named as victor his competitors grew more rebellious. 'Not Toby *again*!' they protested. Some became sullen and gave up, realising quite rightly that they stood little chance against his mastery. Others were spurred to keener resolve and greater cunning. Their hiding places became less obvious and Toby took pleasure in the sport. He had a better idea of the lay of the land now and outhid them at every turn.

The final game was called and a prize announced. The winner would place the candles on Lorelei's cake and light them, then take their seat at the table beside her. Toby felt destiny tap him on the shoulder.

The final count began and the children scattered like excited poultry. Toby took his time. He knew where to go, where to hide. He waited until he was unobserved then slipped downstairs into the dark scullery. He waited a while for his eyes to adjust to the absence of light, then lifted the hatch to the dumb waiter. He slid carefully into the blackness, praying that the lift would take his weight and not plummet into the abyss beneath him. It stood firm and he drew down the hatch, enclosing himself. For this final act of hiding he had a devious idea, one that would ensure his victory. He pulled now at one of the ropes and felt the panelled box rise in its shaft. He pulled again, and again, until the dumb waiter lay between floors. The lifting of a hatch in either the kitchen scullery or the dining room servery above would reveal nothing but an empty shaft. He was part of the floor above and the ceiling below. Neither here nor there. He was hidden in the very heart of the house. His pulse stilled. His breathing slowed. He became calm.

'Is that you, Toby?' said a soft voice beside him.

Toby kicked and thrashed at the panelled walls of the box. He almost called out but checked himself. He was in no danger. He recognised the voice. 'Lorelei?'

'I was hoping it'd be you,' she whispered.

Toby's shock dissipated but his pulse remained quick.

'This is the best hiding place in the whole house,' she confirmed. 'In here we can hide away from everything and everyone, just you and I.'

Toby's imagination was a whirlwind. He feared opening his mouth to speak, so he didn't.

'We can hide away from everyone at the party,' she suggested. 'We can hide from my parents and yours.'

He nodded, unseen.

'We can hide from our teachers and relatives,' she went on. 'We can hide from thunderstorms and piano lessons and algebra and cod liver oil. We can hide from the bullies and the botherers, from the ruffians and the pests. We can hide away from ever having to grow up, from mortgages and income tax, from jealousy and spite and failure and loss. We can hide away from it all.'

Her hand found his. Toby's heart was a moth in a matchbox.

'Don't you wish we could hide here forever Toby?'

This dark, narrow space that smelled of leftovers now seemed the widest paradise. 'Yes,' he croaked.

'Then say it,' she urged him. 'Say: *I wish we could hide here forever.*'

He swallowed. 'I wish we could hide here forever,' he said.

From a far-off room they heard the muffled counting stop. The final search had begun.

Then Toby and Lorelei felt a great dissolution. They crumbled and melted like sugar lumps in hot tea. They fell apart, disintegrating into atoms, into motes and specks and points of light. They drifted into the wainscotting and the oak panelling. They were carried by the faint draughts that blew beneath the doors and through the gaps in the window frames. They settled like dust on the tops of wardrobes and curtain pelmets, on dado rails and the furry heads of stuffed animals mounted on the walls. They threaded themselves into the faded tapestries. They wove themselves into the pile of the hearth rugs and hall runners. They were part of the house now, part of the paint and plaster, part of every brick and tile, every batten, joist and floorboard.

Soon their names would be called. Doors would slam and footsteps would clump about in every corner of the house. The party guests would be sent home, some in tears, others with secret delight at their first taste of scandal.

Tomorrow the grownups would search. There would be sandwiches and smelling salts and the wringing of hands. The cupboards would be emptied and the wardrobes turned out. The men would scour the attic and cellars. The flues would be swept. The hay in the stables would be turned. The woods would be combed and the mere would be dragged.

But Toby and Lorelei would never be found.

Years later, their parents would be laid to rest in their *columbaria* and family mausoleums. In time, everyone they'd ever known would pass.

But the children would remain, two souls entwined, whispering in the dark – a reminder that what is best in us does not always seek the light or walk in the open air.

Sometimes, love hides.

Especially in grand old houses such as this.

10

THE LEPER'S GARDEN

ON THE TINY ISLAND of *Hei Ling Chau* stands the most questionable restaurant in all the world.

La Provençal is the creation of Alphonse Bourdillon, a veteran restaurateur of some renown. His staff, both in the kitchen and in the *salle à manger* are attentive and impeccably trained. The food is exquisite, beyond compare in this part of the world and the cellars brim with a fine line in *Médoc* and *Côtes du Rhône*. Many ingredients are imported and continental recipes are adapted to accommodate the local seafood. The result is inspired, adventurous and always fresh.

The building itself – which dominates the rocky island – was commissioned by Bourdillon himself. With the help of French draughtsmen, architects and interior designers, the restaurant was built and furnished in the most sumptuous tradition of *La Belle Époque*.

The dining area is tiered, and designed to offer every diner at every table a sweeping view of the island and its inhabitants through

153

the tall bow windows that take up one side of the building. Here, clientele may dine in complete luxury and safety, entertained by the island outside. It's this, and not the restaurant's cuisine or standards of service, that calls it into question. What makes La Provençal so questionable is also what makes it such a success.

Because, you see, Hei Ling Chau is no ordinary island.

Hei Ling Chau is a leper colony.

———— ◆ ————

Douglas Opie waits for me at the Star Ferry Pier on Connaught Road. He's not a man to keep waiting. Or in the dark. He studies the clock tower and then my approach. He's suspicious, I can tell. So is Mrs Opie, although her suspicions don't worry me. She's an unimaginative creature and will not be part of this evening's business. The other who waits, however, is the object of all my intentions. She is the reason I have brought them here. She is the one who will lead me from usury and the crooked paths I am forced to walk. She will transform me and, taking my hand in hers, she will usher me into the life I've always desired. Agnes Opie fans herself frantically in the late afternoon humidity. Then she sees me. The fan stills and hides her smile. But I see it gleam in her eyes.

Douglas Opie neglects the hand I offer in greeting and turns to the traffic on Connaught Road. Dust rises from carriage wheels and rickshaws. A gang of coolies sweeps up horse manure. 'Your note didn't explain *why*,' he states.

'Why what?'

'Why La Provençal?'

'Because – there's something I'd like you to see...'

He turns to me. 'What exactly?'

'I'd prefer you saw for yourself,' I say.

'You know what that place *is*?' Mrs Opie looks as if she's just found a fingernail in the *foie gras*.

'I do, madam,' I tell her.

'I'm sure Aubrey has a perfectly good reason.' The fan has fallen from Agnes's face. 'Besides, I've never been. I hear the food is rather good...'

Douglas Opie turns back to Connaught Road with a groan.

It takes over an hour to steam from Central to Hei Ling Chau. Throughout the journey Opie sits opposite, hands on knees, thunder-faced. He's trying to unpick me like a knot, to solve me like a riddle. He's *taipan* of a wealthy trading house but he's from simple stock, risen to riches on the back of his mills and factories in the Midlands. He knows cheap materials when he sees them. His eyes drop to my shoes. I'm embarrassed by their condition. They are old and scuffed to the point that no application of polish might resurrect them. My worn clothes further display my poverty.

Mrs Opie sits beside him, fiddling with the fringes of her parasol. It's impossible to know where her mind is. It could be anywhere in the small, trivial world she inhabits.

Agnes sits next to me. She would loop her arm through mine if it wasn't for the tyranny of her father's gaze. She recounts her week to me instead: tea on the verandah of the Repulse Bay Hotel, a gala at the fencing academy, bridge with mother and her friends. She's trying to be bright about it all.

Across the narrow cabin I lock eyes with Opie.

I can't get off this boat quickly enough.

At Hei Ling Chau the way to the restaurant leads along a narrow stone quay and up an ornate curving staircase. The quay itself, and the approach to the island, is guarded by tall cliffs that isolate visitors from the colony's inmates. Here, diners are quite safe and the quay remains inaccessible as a means of escape for any of the colony's residents. The way is steep, however, and there is still ferocity in the late afternoon sun. Women bundle their skirts for the climb. On the landings the elderly pant for breath, skin shining. Parasols snap open and the youthful streak ahead, laughing, towards the doors of La Provençal.

The climb is worth the effort.

At the very top, waiters parade with trays of iced water in crystal tumblers. Each party is relieved of their hats, then led inside to their appointed table. Expectancy and excitement fizz among the diners as much as a trip to the theatre or the races. Entering the shade of the restaurant Opie takes in the velvet-draped opulence of it all, then returns suspicious eyes to me.

Our table waits in the middle of the room. A white tablecloth, starched and ironed – an armoury of silver cutlery at each setting. Opie flicks his coat-tails to sit and surveys the room with mistrust. The tall bow windows are covered. Long curtains of lace have been drawn across to hide the island from all inside the restaurant. In the filtered light Agnes glows. The climb has brought colour to her cheeks. It's hard not to stare, to drown in her. So warm and alive in this place of disease and despair. My Agnes.

She cocks an eyebrow at me. There's the trace of a smile.

My admiration is too plain and she's sending both a thank-you and a caution. Opie's eyes are on me too.

I take sudden interest in the *bouillabaisse*.

We talk little during the first course. A pall of trepidation is draped about us. Perhaps it is the morbid thrall of the place, of the spectacle soon to be revealed. Perhaps it lies in the not knowing, the questions that each now asks themself. Opie is wondering why on earth he's here. He questions my motives, my character. Agnes wonders if I'll ruin everything. Mrs Opie wonders if there's more bread.

The plates are cleared away and I hear the chime of a wineglass. The head waiter appears and thanks us for our attention. I've heard of this custom. He explains that the lepers of Hei Ling Chau are some of the best cared-for in the world and that our patronage ensures this. A modest amount will be added to each bill in order to provide for them. If we'd like to leave a larger tip, this also goes straight to the island's needy. Our generosity shelters and feeds them. Their meals come from the same kitchen as ours will tonight – a perfect circle of charity. Applause moves through the room. The head waiter announces that the islanders would now like to thank us themselves, in their own way.

Then he bows, and the lace curtains are drawn back.

A low, collective gasp rises in the room. The only other sounds are the wheeling of the curtain tracks and the occasional thump of a wineglass returned too heavily to a table.

Mrs Opie lifts a serviette to her mouth, wide-eyed. 'Are we safe here?' she asks. 'They won't come near us, will they?'

'We're quite safe. Have no fear,' I tell her. Agnes, on the other hand, is unafraid. She looks on with head tilted, mouth slightly open, breathless with fascination.

I watch Opie. Like many in the dining room he stares at the scene beyond the bow windows with an expression of slack-jawed horror. Nearby, several young girls ignore their parents' protests and, laughing, flock to press their noses against the window glass. They giggle and pull faces at the wretches on the other side.

Framed in the window is a pitiful tableau of sickness and desperation. It's a window onto the final stages of the disease, the end of days, the end of hope. This is the detritus of the city, swept from its streets so the wealthy can rest at ease. They stand if they are able, disfigured by sores and dressed in ill-fitting clothes. Each holds a bowl of something. Food? Their evening meal? They raise and drop their arms in the Chinese manner of gratitude, or *kowtow* in the dirt. The effort this takes is plain.

Nurses in white cowls and masks move among them, demanding they thank their benefactors. Others, too far gone to care, sprawl on the rocky, barren ground. Some sit in rough-made litters or prop themselves against rocks. No one eats. I question whether they even have the strength.

Opie rises slowly to his feet. His expression moves from horror to astonishment. He's seen something.

I follow his line of sight to two figures in the centre of the pitiful assembly. One is a man who lies upon a simple bier of wooden planks. He's Chinese but his clothing, although grimy and torn, is Western in fashion and looks as though it was once fine. One trouser leg lies empty, perhaps the result of a recent amputation. Beside him kneels a woman, one hand holding his, the other caressing his brow. But she's white, a European. She wears a green gown, dusty and worn. Her long fair hair obscures her face. She seems to be weeping.

Opie points at them and turns to me with a faltering smile. 'Is that...?'

I nod.

Opie's fascination returns to the couple. He's struggling hard to hide his excitement.

The white woman looks over her shoulder, sensing eyes upon her. I now see how firmly the pestilence has taken hold. Around her slender throat is a necklace of ulcers, black with necrosis. She stands and I see her eyes – knives of bright blue. Her nose is gone from her face. All that is left are two black openings into her skull where her nostrils should be.

She lets the man's hand drop and cradles the heavy mound at her belly. Then she steps towards the window, towards us. I suppress the urge to turn away, to hide my face. *Is she looking at me? Does she see me? Surely not from this distance? And yet, I can see her.*

The woman lifts a finger, pointing in accusation. I see her face flush red with hatred and watch her spit spray as she hurls her curses at the window. The girls pressed against the glass giggle and wave.

Opie saves me. He marches from the table towards the adjoining saloon.

'Douglas. Where are you off to?' bleats Mrs Opie. 'The main course is being served...'

'Hang the mains,' says Opie over his shoulder. 'Aubrey and I will take our brandy and cigars early.' Then he turns to me with newly-minted affability. 'Won't we Aubrey?'

◄—•—►

The smoke from the fine cigar smells like success. It assures me that some business has been concluded this day. Deeds have been done. Pacts have been honoured. In a moment, the plans I have so painfully laid will return their dividends. My brandy waits. I will not touch it until Opie joins me. For now, he seems intent on wearing a path in the Arabic rug. He stops, checks we are alone, then lifts a hand in gesture to the scene we have just witnessed. His voice is a whisper. 'This was *your* doing?'

There. There is the moment.

'It was,' I say.

He shakes his head, amazed. 'But how?'

'If I tell you, you may be considered complicit. It's best if you don't know.'

'But it's too fantastic, I *must* know.'

'And one day I may tell you. But not now, not until all this is forgotten.'

He returns to wearing a rut in the Arabic rug. He has not made his exuberance plain but I can sense it, I can smell it, like the tobacco smoke that drifts across the room. 'How long?' he asks.

'He will not last the week.'

'And his wife, the O'Neill woman?'

'She is in the final stages of the disease. She will not live long.'

Opie's face is clouded with doubt. 'And the child she carries?'

'It will not survive.'

'You are sure?'

'Most sure. The disease will do the work for us. If not, then other arrangements are in place.'

He frowns, unsettled.

'There can be no heir,' I tell him.

He nods in mute acceptance. 'And what of his property, the warehouses at *Shau Kei Wan*?'

'His warehouses are in receivership, as is the cargo they contain,' I explain.

He clasps his hands together and continues to pace. 'So how do I obtain them? Have you a plan for this?'

'I have. There is a magistrate in my debt. I will draft the contracts for sale myself. You will be the only bidder.'

He crosses the room to stand before me. His eyes glitter with expectation. Now he broaches the subject that interests him most. 'And what of the house?'

'Their house at Watergarden stands vacant. There being no heir, it will pass to the Crown.'

'*There being no heir* – what if they've nominated other beneficiaries?' he asks.

'They haven't.'

'You are certain?'

'I drafted their wills myself.'

A smile moves behind his expression. I see a little respect, too – a hard-won sentiment from a man such as Opie.

'We cannot make claim until nature has run its course,' I explain.

'And then?'

'Then I will employ the same means to keep the sale private. I will prepare the contract and you will buy the house for a modest sum.'

'Your magistrate will aid in this?'

'He will adjust certain records on our behalf.'

'And he's deep inside your pocket? You can trust him?'

'He's most keen to wriggle free from the trap I've caught him in.'

Opie throws himself into the chair beside me. He lifts the brandy balloon to his lips and drains it in one. I draw on my cigar and let the tendrils of rich tobacco smoke engulf me. I feel his gaze on me again, a different gaze than before, this time without scrutiny or suspicion. 'It must have cost you time and a pretty penny to bring this about,' he offers.

'It has,' I admit. I don't tell him that the undertaking has driven me to the brink of bankruptcy.

'I hold a man's word more important than anything, don't you?'

I nod.

'Well, you've been true to your word. You've upheld your side of the bargain. Have no fear I'll uphold mine.'

Anticipation dances inside me. I resist letting it show.

His eyes narrow. 'I've misjudged you,' he offers. 'It seems my daughter is a better judge of a man's character than me.'

I smile. 'Well, she's an Opie.'

He laughs. 'Aye, she is that.' For several minutes he falls to introspection and I watch the thoughts tumble behind his eyes. He sees the future now. It's clear. And fortune has kissed both our cheeks.

'What do you think of May?' he asks me.

'May?'

'May is such a fine month for a wedding, don't you think?'

Agnes is overjoyed.

Opie creates a stir by ordering champagne. He wants to treat the entire *salle à manger* in celebration of the engagement. Mrs Opie forbids him. *This must be handled the right way*, she argues. She wants to notify the members of her bridge school first, then an announcement in the *South China Morning Post*. She imagines a guest list for the wedding. She creates a seating plan. She orders flowers. There is talk of *introducing me*. It sounds as if I am to be exhibited in front of the city's elite like a simpering debutante. The idea appals me but I'll comply for Agnes's sake.

On the steamer back to Central Opie beams at me across the narrow cabin, hands on knees. Mrs Opie looks on with a heaving, melodramatic teariness. Agnes loops her arm through mine.

The day has been auspicious and, on the strength of it, tomorrow I will visit a tailor.

And buy myself a new pair of shoes.

The house that Opie has so coveted for all these years is called Watergarden. Situated high on Victoria Peak above Magazine Gap Road it commands views of the city and foreshore. More importantly to him it stands higher on the Peak than all the other lordly dwellings of the trading-house taipans. It's a statement, an act of architectural one-upmanship. From its lofty terraces and casements one can look down on the merchant banks, financiers and administrators of empire. One can thumb one's nose at the entire colony and the lesser souls who inhabit her.

Here, a man is above it all.

The property is owned by one Gabriel Kwan, a wealthy Roman Catholic shipping merchant from Macau. He moved to Hong Kong as a way to escape Chinese commercial controls and, as a result, his business has flourished. In contrast to Opie's approach to commerce (and that of the British generally), Kwan refused to indulge in the lucrative trade of opium. Instead, he's built his company on exports of porcelain, tea, spices and silk. Gabriel Kwan is an outspoken opponent of the opium trade, advocating that no good business can be based on the profits of misery. His views have often drawn him into the firing line of free trade supporters and the particular gunsights of Douglas Opie. Kwan's illness, the resulting collapse of his business and his exile to Hei Ling Chau are all seen as a form of poetic retribution. But the removal of such a competitor is a mere collateral benefit for Opie. Even the seizure of Kwan's warehouses is a side issue. The real prize here is to strip the man of the symbol that elevates him. The symbol that spits in Opie's eye. The pedestal Kwan dares to stand upon – Watergarden House.

The property is worth comment, not so much for the dwelling (which is spacious and comfortable beyond even Opie's needs) but more so for the garden – the water garden itself. A spring opens in the hillside there. Originally this was dammed into a small reservoir but Kwan excavated a cistern of stone to hold larger volumes of water for the drier months. The interior of the cistern is vaulted while the exterior is marked by a flat expanse of stone. To those unfamiliar with the property this looks like an ordinary terrace or patio, except that an iron hand-pump stands at its centre to draw water. Beneath the spout of this pump is an open grate through which can be glimpsed the level of the water deep inside the cistern.

The property's supply of fresh, clean water is abundant. So much so, that the gardens below the house have been terraced into a botanical marvel. An irrigation system feeds the ponds and beds of lotus flowers, water lilies, Chinese willows and camphor trees. On the lowest terraces below the view of the house is a sizeable vegetable garden capable of sustaining the owners and staff of the house throughout the year.

Watergarden House is so named for good reason.

The person who loves these gardens more than anyone is Kwan's wife Kathleen, an O'Neill from County Kerry. This is the woman who now languishes beside him on Hei Ling Chau. Her parents were poor tenant farmers hit hard by the famine. She left Ireland in search of a better life and found purpose in the Catholic Diocese of Hong Kong. She taught English, tended to the poor and sick and, through hard work and tenacity, raised funds for the church's many charities. She is a strong woman, principled, devout, and widely regarded for her kindness and generosity. It was through the church that she met Kwan, a man of similar inclination and qualities.

Once married, she joined her husband at Watergarden House. Here, she expanded the garden, adding further terraces of vegetables and herbs. With the help of her household staff she grew rice, watercress, soya bean and water chestnut, then donated the produce to feed the impoverished. It was her way of giving thanks.

Her own childhood was one of hardship and hunger. This garden is her Eden. Her place of plenty.

Am I sorry for them? Do I regret my part in their ruin? I find it hard to chastise myself. My rise is their downfall. Gain and loss balance the world. It's a simple exchange of power, a law of physics. Perhaps their unborn child is the only innocent victim. And yet, if that child somehow lived it would be nothing more than a halfling, born out of two worlds and an outcast to both. I have done them a service. The child is better off dead.

My intent was never to destroy the Kwans as an end in itself. I am not so evil. They looked on me as a friend, after all. I attended their church, sang their hymns, gave to their poor and helped their needy. They took me in and trusted me, so that when I offered these charitable people the charity of my own experience, they accepted without suspicion. This is how I came to peer into their legal affairs, to write their wills. Be sure – piety, faith and goodness are not strengths in the ways people imagine. They are weaknesses. And even the armour of light has many gaps that can be exploited.

They have been nothing more than instruments to me, rungs in a ladder I will help Opie climb. And, in his climbing, I will climb too. My prize is not a house. It's Agnes. She will open the doors to a new world for me. Beside her, I'll stand above it all, just like Opie will at Watergarden.

⚊●⚊

Agnes Opie carries a small calibre pistol in her purse.

She believes a woman should be equipped to defend herself.

While many of the colony's ladies swelter on croquet lawns or tennis courts, Agnes prefers to take her exercise at the Royal Academy of Fencing. I have watched her compete on several occasions and can confirm that she is both quick and deadly.

Agnes suggests that, once we are married, our domestic disputes are best settled with pistols or foils. This worries me. I have no doubt that, in a fit of ill humour, she has the potential to wound me mortally or run me through.

I think she has a nose for blood.

I once revealed to her that I sometimes gamble at *pai-gau* and *fan-tan* in the local go-downs that sprawl along the waterfront. I'm an infrequent visitor and I don't lose much at the tables because I don't possess much. It's a passing distraction, nothing more.

She begged me to take her there, to the cockfights she'd heard about.

I explained that even if I could wrest her free from the army of chaperones her father employs, she'd be noticed. The task was impossible. She became peevish.

As a consolation I made her a gift of a pair of fighting fish.

She loved them.

These handsome fellows trail their iridescent fins in the same bowl, unaware of each other's presence. They are separated by an opaque screen of green onyx which may be lifted from the bowl at a whim.

Agnes ran a finger across the top of this screen, asking me what would happen if she removed it.

'They'll tear each other to pieces for you,' I said.

Her eyes shone. 'They shall be my gladiators,' she announced. '*Morituri te salutant.*'

I saw her clearly then – an empress of antiquity sat on her throne high above the blood-soaked sands of the arena.

In her lovely hands she balances the scales of life and death.

There is a cruelty in Agnes Opie that excites me.

I dream of the time we might at last be alone.

— ◆ —

One of the worst things about being a lawyer is also the most useful.

Although we serve the well-to-do, we also get to swim in the sewers with the rats. We see the world from beneath. We keep the counsel of kings and cut-throats alike.

When local undesirables run smack into the British legal system it's me they appeal to for help. In this, I've cultivated something of a reputation. I've saved Pearl River pirates from the noose and defended smugglers, slavers and insurrectionists. Criminal families have pledged themselves in my debt. I never charge for my services and this enhances my reputation. Although it keeps me poor, it pays in other ways. I am owed, and the few favours I ask in return are never denied.

When Opie strayed into my orbit I conceived a way to give him his heart's desire in exchange for my own.

I called in my credit and spread word. I was on the lookout for a certain breed of person – a weapon, a deliverer who would bring ruin to the house of Kwan and grant me favour with the house of Opie.

The answer came in the form of a *Hakka* woman. A destitute. I never knew her name.

The Hakka people are a hardy race of seafarers and farmers. They do not bind their women's feet. Yet Hakka women are best identified by another characteristic: their unique *laang-mo* hat. This hat of bamboo and straw differs little from the hats worn by other

Chinese except that from its wide brim hangs a veil of black cloth. The veil protects the wearer's face from sun, weather and insects.

In this poor woman's case it also hid the ravages of leprosy.

I employed her to visit Watergarden House to beg. She arrived, wearing her traditional black tunic and trousers, her face covered. To her chest she clutched her only belongings, a bundle wrapped in rags. Falling prostate on the steps of the garden gate, she wept, she pleaded for help. She was starving and alone. She'd heard of the merciful white woman whose gardens overflowed with fruit and vegetables. She'd heard stories of generosity and compassion, and begged to be made known. Kathleen was informed and came to the gate herself. She lifted the poor soul to her feet and made her welcome.

Take heed. This is how virtue lays us open. The meek do not inherit the earth. They are preyed upon by the ambitious, by the strong.

For two days and a night, the Hakka woman remained inside the walls of Watergarden. She was fed, she slept in a bunk in the servants' halls, never parted from the precious bundle of rags she held. She was encouraged to rest and given the liberty of the grounds, to wander the terraces and garden. She was last seen standing beside the iron pump, her bundle still clutched to her chest. She was staring into the grate above the cistern.

When she left the house, the bundle in her arms was gone.

⫷ ● ⫸

Months later the dead child in the cistern was found.

One of the gardeners, taking a break to drink from the iron

pump, saw something floating in the water below. He and his colleagues lowered ropes and bale hooks into the cistern. The bundle was retrieved and unwrapped. No more than a newborn, the child had likely never drawn breath. It was rotten with leprosy, and the contagion had already done its work.

The household staff succumbed first, then Gabriel Kwan became bedridden. Kathleen tended him for as long as she was able. She took over his business affairs as best she could while the house was placed in quarantine. No one offered help. The Kwans were a people apart. Neither Chinese nor European, they were foreigners to all. And so the world turned its back.

Payments were missed, cargoes remained unloaded. Crews went without wages and left their ships at anchor or abandoned them in the docks. My enterprising friends in the Pearl River were happy to help. They raided Kwan's vessels and scuttled them. In time the excisemen moved in. Then the bank. Then the bailiffs. As Kwan drifted closer to death, his business drifted into ruin.

At the end, he and Kathleen were left all alone at Watergarden House. The most loyal among their staff, the ones who remained, became infected and were sent to Hei Ling Chau. Then the disease took hold of Kathleen, too. Stubborn woman. She kept vigil at her husband's bedside until she was no more than a walking corpse. She shuffled and limped around that huge, dark house all by herself. She harvested what remained in the dwindling, overgrown garden to keep her husband from death's door. I drafted the court order and my indebted magistrate signed it.

In the dead of night, Gabriel and Kathleen were spirited away to Hei Ling Chau, reunited with their dying servants.

I arranged for the house to be fumigated. The cistern was opened and flushed with lime. I paid for a chemist from Strasbourg to conduct examinations. After many weeks and many rigorous tests in his laboratory he pronounced the water untainted. In evidence of this he even drank a pitcherful himself. To my knowledge he is still in excellent health.

———◆———

'I'm not in favour of this,' says Opie. He sits with a stormy look at his desk in the study at Watergarden. At his back the tall casement window frames the sweep of his conquest from the Peak to Victoria Harbour. Beyond the nine mountains, China crouches in the haze.

'I understand, but I'll return in four to five months,' I say.

'I'd prefer to keep you close.' Whether he means this for his own sake or his daughter's is unclear.

Opie did not make me ambitious, nor did Agnes. I've always been this way. After all, this is why a man endures the Orient, this is why a man comes here. Like many, I ride the coat-tails of empire, drifting in the wake of Palmerston's gunboats as they open up a new continent of opportunity. There's plenty of work for a lawyer in the treaty ports of Canton, Amoy and Shanghai. There are trade agreements to be ratified and contracts to be signed. There's much to do for a swimmer among rats. 'You realise I have obligations?' I tell Opie.

'You have obligations here,' he replies.

'I'm aware. But there's business I'm to conclude first in the treaty ports. I cannot escape my legal obligations there without consequence,' I urge him. 'There are too many people I'm indentured to, too many agreements I cannot break. Just a few months and I'll return.'

He draws a long breath, his eyes fixed on mine. 'Then go conclude your business and wind up your affairs,' he instructs.

'Wind up my affairs?' The impertinence of his directive lands like a slap across my face.

'Dissolve your business,' he orders.

'Why?'

'You won't need it.' His face softens a little. 'I'll give you a new one, if you're open to the idea.'

Intrigue uncoils inside me. I feel a smile rise to my face. 'Go on...'

'I have a use for men like you – resourceful men, men with a certain *ingenuity*. Face it Aubrey, you're wasted at the fringes of empire.' He waves a dismissive hand. 'Let the vultures be the first to feed, the dullard military men and merchants. Let them dig in the mud for their spoils. Come join me on the mountaintop and have it all.' He leans towards me, across his desk. 'Besides, I want my son-in-law *here*.' He directs a finger at the centre of his desk. 'With my daughter.'

'What do you offer?' I ask.

'Legal Director of my company and a seat on the board.'

I search his face. He's serious. I'd hoped that, in time, I could win him over, bring him to consider an offer such as this. But *so soon*? I picture a gilded door standing open. Agnes is on my arm, and I am about to enter the glittering, pompous decadence that lies at the centre of the world. 'I accept,' I say without further thought. I have no idea how I might look, what my expression might betray. I suspect I look stupefied, overwhelmed by the immensity of what is now unfolding.

'Wind up your affairs and come back to us,' commands Opie. He gets to his feet, turns to the casement window and gazes over his dominion. 'My wife has plans for the garden, you know.'

'Oh?' I offer. My mind is elsewhere.

'She plans to dig up those Chinese weeds, the ones they have the hide to call *vegetables*.'

I hear his words but their meaning does not touch me.

'She wants to plant roses. A capital idea, but I'm not sure roses will benefit from such wet feet.' He turns to me. 'What do you think?'

I am not in the same room. I am not even the same person.

Suddenly I am a man with an enviable wife and few concerns. I no longer grovel and scheme for a living. I can leave the swimming with rats to others now. I live in luxury, sheltered in the bosom of one of the East's largest trading houses. I am son-in-law to Douglas Opie and one day I will be taipan of Watergarden House.

———◆———

'I'll be back in time for the wedding *banns*.' I try to reassure Agnes.

She stands at the foot of the gangplank, her opened parasol rests on her shoulder. She wears a bright new dress but her look is dark. Even in such a mood, she's ravishing. 'I'll be so *bored*,' she complains. 'You have no idea. You're deserting me for adventure, sentencing me to months of bridge clubs and tea parties. It'll be hell.'

'You'll manage,' I tell her.

'I hate you,' she says.

'And I love you,' I say, kissing her cheek. 'And when I come back, I'll be back for good. I promise.'

'I might not wait that long,' she says.

'You'd take another?'

'Perhaps,' she says. 'What would you do?'

'I'd buy myself a pistol and learn its use,' I say.

'You'd fight for me?'

'To the death.'

A serpentine smile lifts the corner of her lips.

'I'll write you,' I say. 'Will you write me back?'

She twirls her parasol. 'Perhaps,' she says.

— • —

Of course she writes. She writes so often that it lifts me from the drudgery of these last few tasks I undertake in service of the man I once was.

I cannot wait to leave here, to fly back to her on the first ship and gaze again on the reckless, selfish beauty of her. I cannot wait to claim all that is mine and begin the life I have conceived. My work will soon be done. The gilded door to that other life is within reach. Soon I will grasp its handle and, turning it, I will step inside.

She writes complaining of her father's over-protectiveness. Opie has increased his vigilance it seems, but only to make Agnes feel imprisoned. She asks me for my legal opinion as to whether '*shooting a chaperone through the leg might have repercussions?*' I write back, replying that such an act would be '*inadvisable and technically a crime punishable by law*'.

She believes the act is warranted as a means of self-defence.

She tells me she's being held against her will.

Agnes complains of the social gauntlet her mother makes her run. Her bridge club friends are haranguing her over Agnes's choice of wedding couturier. At her mother's insistence plans are changed. Tempers flare. They argue over the list of wedding guests. Agnes barricades herself in her room. Her mother is reduced to tears. They make amends over sponge cake and Darjeeling on the verandah of the Repulse Bay Hotel. It's a temporary truce. Tempers flare again over the choice of reception venue. Agnes believes her mother is treating the wedding as if it's her own. Her mother believes Agnes is self-centred. Watergarden House is filled with the screams of mother and daughter. Opie works late at his office in town. The servants hide.

In *Hankow* I receive a short, abrupt missive: '*Come home now!*' it reads. I write back with all the tenderness I can summon. I miss her. I love her. I will return soon. I promise.

For several weeks I receive no word. No letter. I worry that Agnes is offended, or that rage for her family now somehow extends to me. I suspect her of being bitter because I'm not there to defend her, not there to take her side.

Then she writes.

> *Dearest Aubrey,*
> *I have not revealed this until now because I did not wish to cause alarm.*
> *But now I must. It's the only thing that consumes my waking thoughts and my sleepless nights. I am so afraid.*
> *Watergarden House is haunted. I am sure of it.*

Do not despair. My grip on reality has not slipped. I am the same, I am healthy and whole. But, my God, the things I have seen. Others have seen them too. I pray that tomorrow you might return to me and that we might leave this gloomy house forever.

The phantom visits at night. I have seen it walk the terraces of the garden and stand near the grate above the cistern. It moves from room to room and through the empty halls. I have woken freezing in the hot night, terrified by some nameless fear, only to see the apparition standing at the foot of my bed. Then my heart kicks in my chest like a spring foal.

One evening after supper Mother screamed the house down claiming she'd seen a ghastly figure watching her through a window.

Then she fainted, falling to the drawing room floor.

Father had one of the maid's feet beaten for lacing Mama too tightly, but I know the truth. She'd seen the same apparition as me – a woman dressed in black, her face covered by a veil. She carries a small bundle in her arms.

I am so very frightened, Aubrey. Hurry back to me. I need you.

Agnes.

My hand shakes as I place the letter on my desk. Agnes's spring foal now kicks in my own chest.

Under regular circumstances I'd explain all this away for her. I'd put it down to her anxieties over the forthcoming wedding, her frustrations with her mother. Their arguments. Her isolation and over-chaperoned confinement. Pressures such as these can disarrange even the most ordered mind.

But I'm reeling from the details. They're too specific. *A veiled figure dressed in black? A bundle in her arms?*

Then there's the business of standing over the grate to the cistern.

I refuse to believe such things are in this world, things beyond the scope of science, beyond reason. There is a better explanation, and yet, how much better could such an explanation be? I bring my hands to my face. In this damp, relentless heat I am greasy with sweat. I walk a circle in my rented room.

Who knows?

Who is trying to punish me?

Is it a warning? A message? Is this a precursor to blackmail? I shudder at this possibility because it's the only sane explanation I can land on. Yet the Hakka woman had no family. I never met her but only spoke to her through a go-between who knew her tongue. There were no witnesses, there is no link between her and me. I was most careful. So which rat that I swam with now seeks to eat at my table? In truth there are so many that I forget. Was there someone I offended? Were any of my demands in excess of the services I'd provided? Who's behind this? Whose hand now turns the rack on which I lie?

But it's all too elaborate. Why would anyone, even the most vindictive, the most hateful of villains go to such lengths? I'm confounded. I throw myself into a chair, take up my pen and begin to write Agnes a reply. My words are a scrawl, my hand will not stop shaking. I do not write of ghosts, I do not humour her or go so far as to tell her that I believe her. I only implore her to look to her own safety, to be wary of those around her, to look for signs of deceit and devilry among the living. I ask her to watch and listen. To be my eyes and ears. She will learn the truth for me.

And we will root the culprit out.

⎯⎯ ● ⎯⎯

The steam packets that ply the five hundred mile length of the Yangtze river from Shanghai to Hankow are the only connection to the world outside. As such, the most precious goods they carry are not whisky, silver or gunpowder but newspapers and letters – news from the world we have left behind. The vessels are built for speed and cargo space. For this reason they are lightly armed. This makes them a desirable target for privateers and rebels. They are often fired upon by cannon from the banks of the river or blockaded and boarded. For over a month there is no contact with the outside world. When a packet finally arrives, under naval escort, we rejoice. But there are no letters for me. Nothing from Watergarden. Were they lost in previous shipments? Is there something I was supposed to have done but did not act upon? Is there some question I did not answer? I have no way of knowing. All I know is that now, the letters stop coming. Month after month, packet after packet, I receive no word from Agnes. Does she punish me too? Am I rejected, or has something happened at Watergarden?

For the first time, my fingers rest uncertainly on the handle to that gilded door. I have no idea what lies beyond it now.

Leaving unfinished business, I flee Hankow. There's more to

178

be done in the other treaty ports but I make my apologies on the grounds of ill health. I'll suffer financial losses and notoriety but I don't care. I'm desperate to know what's happened at home.

Home – is that the way I think of Watergarden now? I suppose it is, and I will not, *cannot* tolerate any threat to it, to my future security, or the life I have fought so hard to become a part of.

Three weeks later, and after an absence of five long months I step from a gangway onto Hong Kong's familiar quay stones.

I am here. Let the truth unfold.

◄—•—►

'There's a message fer ye...' says my articled clerk. He waits for me quayside, wringing his cap. He's a scruffy, big-boned lad with untameable red whiskers. He'll never get beyond his articles, he's not that bright. But he's straight as a pound of candles and he's all I can afford.

'Well?' I hold out my hand.

He blushes. 'Oh, 'tis not that *sort* of message,' he says. ''Twas *spoken.*'

'By who?' I ask him.

'A lady, sir, who visited chambers today. She said...' At this he clears his throat. 'You may see your fiancée tonight at La Provençal. A table is reserved.'

Relief suffuses me. I had waited so long to hear news of Agnes, that she is well. This is the best welcome home I could wish for – dinner at the restaurant where I'd been promised her hand. A fitting return. I hope that this evening she will give her family and chaperones the slip. I am about to ask how she appeared – was she healthy, was she happy? My clerk prevents me. He flashes an urgent look along the waterfront to the Star Ferry Pier and says, 'Last ferry's about to leave, sir. I'd hop to it if I were ye.' He returns his well-wrung cap to his head and tugs the peak. 'I'll look to yer luggage...'

I've been denied civilised company for so long. I've become lazy with my grooming. My fears for Agnes have consumed me and I am tired from the voyage. I know this shows in my bearing and every line of my face. Now I drip with perspiration from my race along the waterfront. A deckhand holds the mooring line while I leap aboard the ferry. I don't care how I look. I drop into a seat and smile in triumph. Agnes will forgive my appearance. There'll be no more partings, no more goodbyes between us. This evening will be a sweet reunion.

The steamer takes an eternity to reach Hei Ling Chau, even longer than that first intolerable journey while I sat pinned by Opie's gaze. I call on the craft to move more quickly, I will the waves to assist us, I beseech the wind to push at our stern.

We dock and I'm the first to jump ashore. I run towards the curving staircase and bound upwards, two steps at a time. At the top I pause to catch my breath. I drink a glass of water and wipe my brow. I give my name. A waiter ushers me inside.

The sudden change from bright afternoon sunshine to the dim interior of the restaurant causes me a temporary blindness. The lace curtains remain drawn across the bow windows. I keep my eye on the waiter and follow him. We arrive at a table for two and he pulls out a chair, gesturing for me to sit. A woman is seated opposite. She is dressed in the weeds of a widow, a black veil over her face. 'There must be some mistake,' I say, searching the room for Agnes.

'There is no mistake,' says the widow. Her voice is a rasp, the scuttling of insects.

The waiter holds the back of the chair and rolls his eyes towards its cushioned seat with entreaty.

'But I'm here to see my fiancée,' I explain.

'And see her you will,' says the widow. 'Sit, please.'

Confused, I do as I am bid.

'I'm glad you accepted my invitation,' she says.

'*Your* invitation? Do I know you?' I ask.

'How quickly you've forgotten,' she replies. There is something in her voice, beneath the rattle and scrape of it that lifts and falls like a forgotten lullaby. In the light of the table lamp I can see she is wealthy. Her mourning clothes are of fine black silk, embroidered and ruched. She wears a necklace of black pearls that catches and splits the lamplight. A black-gloved hand rests on the silver hilt of a walking cane.

I lean close. She turns to me. Through her veil's black lace I see the flash of her eyes – knives of bright blue. Two dark cavities loom where her nose should be.

I recoil, my chair screeching across floorboards. '*Kathleen*?' I cry.

I am hissed at from a nearby table. The head waiter is addressing the gathered diners from the centre of the salle à manger. The waiter pauses, frowning in my direction.

Her bright eyes retreat into darkness. 'Have no fear, I am no longer infectious,' she whispers. 'The disease has left me.'

'How in the Devil's name...?' I stammer.

'The Devil had nothing to do with it.' Her lilting, Irish accent rings clear now. 'It was a poor fishing family from Lantau Island. I once nursed their son through typhus. I brought him back to health. In return they saved me. They carried me away from here.' She tilts her head in examination of me. 'Kindness begets kindness, Aubrey. Whereas evil only begets evil.'

Her mention of my name is a plunge into cold water.

'There's a monastery on Lantau, did you know that? The monks have ways with the disease that surpass our own. When I'd recovered I returned to Macau, to my husband's home. We have family and still a little wealth hidden away there.' She produces a handkerchief and lifts it beneath her veil, to her mouth. Her cough is a death rattle.

'Where is Agnes?' I repeat, looking about. I'm stricken, desperate, and something about this meeting crawls over me like the cold shivering of fever.

'Your magistrate is arrested, do you know?' she offers.

I shake my head.

'He's caged, poor little bird. You should hear how sweetly he sings.'

I feel my mouth fall open.

'I wonder where you'll run dear Aubrey? There are not enough dark holes in this wide world to hide you. The law has begun its work. Soon I'll claw back all I've lost. My husband will never return to me but I'll recover his warehouses, his scuttled ships, his lost cargoes and more besides. I'll strip that murderer Opie to the bone.'

'I must see Agnes. Where is she?' Panic fails inside me.

Her whisper is edged with menace. 'I'll take back the house, too. Although, Watergarden was never really *his*. It was a wicked thing you did, Aubrey – helping them steal my home. The house is mine by right. You remember – *there being no heir*? Well, *I* am heir, I always have been, as would have been my...'

I am struck with a sudden memory – the rounded belly she cradled, even in the most crippling throes of the disease. The halfling to be, her and Gabriel's successor. I finish her sentence for her. 'Your child?'

The figure in black seems to shrink, the silk mourning dress crumples as if there's no one inside. 'My daughter...' she begins. Her thin voice vibrates with grief. She sits in silence for some time, head bowed, her gaze fixed on the white tablecloth and glittering cutlery. The veil hides her tears, no doubt, as is its purpose.

'She was born leprous,' Kathleen continues. 'She lived one precious day for me, then she was called to God.'

She brims with pain. With rage, too. Somehow these are one, a binary emotion that turns upon itself, feeding on its own power. A serpent eating its own tail.

'She would have loved the garden,' Kathleen says, her voice breaking. 'She would have loved to dirty her hands in soil alongside me, to plant, to nurture, to grow. After she died I took her there. I took her home. I still have a key, so I showed her the glory of the terraces and gardens. I showed her the grand house she might have lived in. I showed her the room that might have been hers.'

The machinery of thought turns, then falls into place like thunder, as if all the locks in some dark, echoing tower have turned as one and every door stands open. Now I understand.

The figure in black that haunted Watergarden was no apparition returned from beyond a Chinese grave. It was a living visitor in different clothes, European clothes – *widow's weeds*? It was another veil that hid this spectre's face, a different bundle that she clutched.

'The phantom was you!' My accusation is too loud. I am hissed and jeered at. At an adjacent table a man calls to me to be silent.

'No phantom,' she whispers. 'Just wounded flesh and poisoned blood.'

I recall Agnes's letter, her recounting of the figure standing over the grate beside the pump, holding its bundle. 'And your daughter,' I begin to ask, fearing the answer. 'Where is she now?'

'In death she gave me one last gift, one final act of love.'

I shake my head, tears spring to my eyes. 'Where is she?'

'I gave her to the cistern,' says Kathleen.

I clap my hand to my mouth. Or my cry would shake the island.

'The way your assassin did,' she says.

I drop my hand. 'Where is Agnes?' I demand again, looking to left and right. The commotion around me grows more hostile. A waiter begs me to be quiet.

Kathleen lifts a black-gloved forefinger to her lips. I fall silent, my eyes fixed on those knives of bright blue. I hear the wheeling of curtain tracks as sunlight floods the room. Kathleen's finger falls from her face and points towards the light, in the direction of the bow window. I follow it.

The familiar, collective gasp rises in the room. The curtains stand drawn, as if revealing the opening scene to some theatre of the

11

THE HARE BRIDE

Never pass a witch-hare by,
Nor dare to look her in the eye,
But rend your garments neck to hem,
Then start your journey once again.

I HAVE NEVER SEEN so many animals inside a church.

Not even at Harvest Festival, or the Feast of Saint Francis.

Today they are gathered for a different reason – for a *funeral*.

And it's just as Billy would have wished.

On the pew beside me, a little girl casts me a smile from below the brim of her bonnet. She is making a poor job of comforting the spring lamb she holds. A boy in his Sunday best sits next to her with a basket on his lap. Within it, a kitten mauls his fingers.

Elsewhere, obedient farm dogs sit at their master's feet, children hold pet rabbits or wicker cages filled with chicks. A donkey foal is tethered to a pillar in the transept. It stands uneasily on the hard stone flags. There are calves, piglets, ducks and geese.

The women of the parish carry their angry toy dogs or colourful birds in cages. One of their number sits with defensive arms wrapped around a glass bowl. Inside it swims a pair of golden fish.

I sing loudly, as we all do, to raise my voice above the bleating, clucking, barking, lowing and braying.

All things bright and beautiful,

All creatures great and small...

But the animals are louder.

I almost laugh to think that they too are lifting their voices in praise.

Even without the animals the church has people enough. Every seat is filled and those standing line the walls shoulder-to-shoulder. People cram into the South Aisle, they stand in the vestry doorway and squeeze into the West Tower. From as far as the Devon border they have come. I recognise members of the Anti-Whaling League, the anti-fur trade lobby, the fox-hunting abolitionists, the Friends of Creation, the trap and snare protesters and the Humane Society. Each has come to pay their respects to the once gentle and benevolent man who now lies in an oak casket on the chancel step.

How fitting, it seems, that the place in which I should see him last was also the place I saw him first – on the path outside this very church. I was just a boy then, and he already a young man. He was a frightening sight – a soul spat straight from the bowels of the earth. His hair was matted with mud, his skin filthy with the loam and arsenic of the mine. He wore a fresh jacket and a badly knotted tie over the rags that clothed the rest of him.

Never have I seen a man so wild and woebegone. And sorrow never left those eyes from that day on.

How appropriate also that today would be his eighty-first birthday. That a man should be laid to rest on the day he first drew breath has a completeness, a *rightness* to it. His life was now neatly folded, like a freshly pressed shirt placed back inside our Maker's drawer.

Billy died quietly in his bed just three days ago. Three days before his birthday. And Billy's birthday falls on the third day of the third month.

Three, times three, times three.

Now, as you and I both know, *three* is a magic number.

Yet numbers were not the only way in which the life of Billy Tresize was touched by magic.

◄—●—►

To the west of Sancreed village, on the road that leads over the windy moorland towards St. Just, stands the house where Billy grew up.

The house is simple, hard and ungracious – much like the people who have called it home. Just four small rooms in all. To its eastern side, shielded from the Atlantic gales, lies a goodly sized walled garden with an iron gate that opens to the countryside beyond. The garden was intended for vegetables, but in Billy's youth was sown with only weeds and a single barren apple tree. In one corner stood a coop where an indignant hen refused to lay eggs.

Billy's father worked the mines of Botallack and Boswedden. He was a *hard rock man*, one who slipped between the cracks of granite deep inside the earth to follow the seams of tin and copper. At five o'clock every morning, he climbed aboard the mine captain's wagon and came home after dark. If he had the price of a pint of ale in his pocket he'd spend it at the Moon and Sixpence.

Billy's mother worked for the mines too. Not below ground like his father, but above, as a maiden of the mine, a *bal-maiden*. She separated the ore with hammer and hand. There was good money in it, more than gutting fish or scratching a living from the land.

Now, whether she neglected to wear her towser and mask, or chose not to dip her hands in protective clay as many of the bal-maidens did, shall never be known. But, bit by bit, the arsenic got to her, either from the ore in her hand or the mineral dust in the air. First her hands turned black, and then her face. Then the tremors came. She began to spit blood as her lungs yielded to consumption. Billy would have been no more than ten years old.

When his mother became bedridden and fought for every breath, Billy's father made an assessment and decided in his own favour. One day he was gone, as if he'd slipped between a crack in the granite into darkness forever. The rumour was that he travelled overseas, like so many hard rock men did. Their skills were highly valued in the mines of the Americas and Africa. In such places a miner could live like a prince, so they said.

Young as he was, Billy was a sturdy one, with hair as red as a roof-tile and shoulders broad enough for labour and responsibility alike. He took it on himself to be breadwinner and walked the five miles to Botallack. As a son of miners he was admitted to the mine's employ. But even at his tender age he was not permitted to work above ground alongside the bal-maidens. This would make a boy soft, it was feared, and bring out the mother in the women. So, every day, Billy met the captain's wagon and descended into darkness like his father before him. He crawled through gaps and along fissures to lay charges in places the men could not reach. He swept the filthy, narrow flues and ventilation shafts. Eventually, he became stable-lad for the pit ponies – a job he grew to love. The ponies were stabled in some of the deepest adits and galleries of the mine. They were winched down as foals and would never be winched out. Each day they were worked to exhaustion, never seeing sunlight or tasting green grass. Billy named each one and comforted the animals when the men were blasting. He brought them carrots and apples as treats from the world above, and was quick to reproach any miner who treated them cruelly, even at the risk of a shovel haft across his back.

Misfortune brought Billy back to the surface. In the gentlest terms, the doctor explained that his mother would not recover. Hers would be a slow downhill path towards the grave. The best Billy could do was to help her make the journey in peace. Laudanum was prescribed, as was an emollient for the skin and vapours to ease her breathing. She could no longer be left alone. Billy tended her day and night but in his heart he felt she had already left. In devoting himself to her care he could no longer work. Without his wage from the mine, the mutton and beef that once went into the pot became turnip and cattle-beets. The wheat that once made the bread became millet and grass seed. Driven by hunger, Billy often marched into the walled garden ready to stretch the indignant hen's neck. But he never did. Instead, he offered it a portion of his own millet in apology for his thoughts. Then the coal ran out. First the hearth grew cold, and then the range for cooking. Light and warmth fled the house like an unscrupulous tenant.

As Billy and his mother drifted closer to starvation, help came from the *Women's Mission*. Each week, a procession of flint-faced, black-clothed women descended upon the Tresize house with parcels of clothing, food, lamp-oil, and coal. Billy was forced to repay their kindness with hours upon his knees in prayer. He prayed for crimes he was unaware he'd committed. He prayed for his mother; that she be restored to health. He prayed for his father, too. Billy also suspected that animals might have souls and so he prayed for the ponies in the pit. He even prayed for the eternal soul of the indignant hen.

The mission women declared that his predicament was his own making. Sinfulness and laziness were the causes. They set him to work with a bucket, brush and broom. Billy guessed their generosity was given in service of their own piety as much as sympathy. He endured their chastisement to keep his mother as comfortable as he might, and himself on the better side of death's door. He was bound to his mother's misery as much as he was bound to the charity of the Women's Mission. He felt trapped, like a pony in a pit; tethered in darkness to a life he could not escape.

If his mother slept, and if the women of the mission left him alone for long enough, he'd slip outdoors. Just for a while. He'd find freedom in the high country to the west of the village – in the treeless, windswept beauty of Caer Bran. An iron-age hilltop fort had once stood there. All that remained were the grassy barrows and the giant, circular scars of the ditch and ramparts. In his mind, Billy rebuilt the palisades and gate. He smelled the smoke of the watch-fires and the forge. He walked the muddy tracks between the crowded stone dwellings and heard the whispers of the ancient ones inside.

The summit of Caer Bran offered views across the countryside to every point of the compass and the sea in three directions. To the north, the Celtic Sea with Ireland hidden in the mist; to the south, the English Channel. To the west lay the broad, stormy prospect of the great Atlantic. Caer Bran was the top of Billy's world, a place he could be raised above the hardship and sorrow of life below.

One day, while searching for nettles and mugwort to make tea, here among the grassy barrows he found her.

◄ ● ►

The doe-hare was caught around the foreleg by a snare, doubtless intended for the neck of a rabbit. Instead, it had somehow foul-trapped the unfortunate animal. Sensing its death, the hare screamed. It kicked and pulled as Billy approached. He removed his jacket and threw it over the creature. Then, when it had calmed, he laid hands upon it, holding it firmly. He loosened the trap's cruel constriction and inspected the wound. The wire had cut deep. The poor animal's foreleg was like a sock ready to be pulled from the bone. Billy wrapped his jacket more tightly around the wounded hare. Then he picked her up and carried her home.

Billy had only seen rabbits before – soft, rounded animals, slow and dull. This hare was unlike any rabbit. She was lean and charged with awareness and energy. Her legs were long, made for speed. She was a courser, a sprinter; swiftness made flesh. Strangest of all, her fur was entirely white, her eyes red as rubies. Billy knew she was no white hare at all, but a colourless one, as if she had speed enough to outrun even colour itself.

He bathed the wound and dressed it. Then he gave her bread soaked in milk, and a little of the cattle-beets. He wrapped the animal in a blanket and held her in his lap as he sat before the fire. The hare dozed and Billy dozed too. When he awoke, she was gone. He guessed she'd sought a dark corner in which to hide, but was glad to find her in the middle of the parlour, eating the beets he'd left. The hare studied him with a sidelong look. A single, ruby eye burned in his direction, assessing him. Billy believed that this was an intelligent creature and that the animal understood he meant no harm.

As he went about his work tending his mother, the hare was wont to follow. It walked after him in ungainly strides – first its two forelegs stretched out, then the hind ones followed. The animal was not created to move slowly. She would only be graceful at speed. While he worked at the chopping board or range, the hare sat patiently, studying him with a sidelong ruby eye.

Each day, Billy checked and dressed the hare's wound. Each day, she grew stronger, as did the bond between them. At night, she would sit in his lap beside the fire. He marvelled at the long white fur around her throat and at the ends of her paws. He named her *Cloudfoot*.

There was no one in Billy's life he could call a friend. He had never been to school, never owned a pet, and was growing up as an only child in an adults' world. Cloudfoot was the closest thing to a companion he'd ever known.

The following wet Tuesday saw a visit from two of the mission women. They flew through the pelting rain like black-cloaked emissaries of penitence and misery. Billy had been tending to his mother. He came downstairs to watch the visitors flap and flail from their rain-wet overcoats and unpin their soaked hats. The first of them carried her dripping garments into the parlour, most likely to dry them beside the fire. She stopped and dropped her bundle to the floor. With a gasp, she retreated and crossed herself, mumbling. In the centre of the parlour sat Cloudfoot. The woman tried backing through the parlour door just as her companion tried to enter. The door was scarcely wide enough for one of them, let alone two women moving in opposite directions, so the door frame made temporary prisoners of them both. The second of the pair noticed Cloudfoot with a shriek. Then the two women left the house as quickly as they had entered. Billy stepped past the bundle of wet clothing on the floor and watched from the window. Hatless, coatless, the two women ran through the rain towards the village, glancing over their shoulders. Billy hung the wet coats and hats in the hallway.

Cloudfoot's wound healed fully, and Billy untied the dressing. Around the same time, things began to happen in the Tresize home.

First, the indignant hen began to lay, just a single egg each week, but then increasing to an egg almost every day. Next, the barren apple tree flowered and bore fruit. Then, without tilling or sowing, the walled garden brought forth broad beans, rhubarb, cabbage, carrots, turnip and potatoes. A bush that once appeared to be a weed now hung with plump damsons, and the sparse vines that covered the trellises of the walled garden flourished with logan-berries, and espaliers of figs and pomegranates.

Billy put all this down to the warmer weather as summer approached. However, this could not explain other happenings. The coal bunker never seemed to empty. The windows gleamed without cleaning, and if Billy left a dirty dish on the parlour table at night, it was washed, dried and put away in the kitchen dresser by morning.

This could only mean that the house was still invaded from time to time, albeit secretly, by the women of the mission. Yet the black overcoats and hats, now dry, still hung from a peg in the hallway. They were never collected.

One evening as nightfall crept from the east, Billy closed the window in his mother's room against the chill and lit her lamp. He noticed that the hump-backed tambour clock upon her mantle had stopped – just recently, he judged by the hour. He wound the key and tapped the movement, but the familiar click of cog and ratchet refused to sound. Instead, Billy heard something that drifted to his ears from downstairs – a woman's voice, humming a song he thought he knew.

He found her in the chair before the parlour fire, her back towards him. Her long hair was not pinned ruthlessly into compliance like that of a mission woman. It hung in a single, loose knot on the nape of her neck, tawny and shot with threads of gold in the firelight. Billy stepped around the chair to see her face. She was more youthful than the others, taller too, long-limbed and far more fair.

The young woman looked up from the beans she'd been shelling in a bowl on her lap. Without turning, she cast him a sidelong look. A single eye burned in Billy's direction. 'Ah, there you are, Billy Tresize,' she said.

'Am I to begin my prayers now?' asked Billy.

'Only if you feel the need.'

Billy looked to left and right. 'Then should I sweep or scrub?' he asked.

'The house looks clean enough,' said the young woman.

Billy met the gaze of the bright, sidelong eye. 'Then what would you have me do?'

Her mouth curled into a smile. 'Come sit with me awhile.' She tapped a footstool with the sole of her shoe.

As she worked, she asked Billy about himself – had he ever been to Sunday School, did he know his letters and his numbers, could he write, what stories did he like, was there a girl he courted?

Never had anyone been so interested in him. As she charmed the answers from him he was snared by the warm smile and the eyebrow cocked in question. She asked him if he would like to learn the alphabet and how to use numbers to his advantage. There was safer employment above ground for men who knew such things, she said.

The evening grew late, but the fire did not burn low, and the light from the window did not dim. Billy could not remember a time he had talked at such length with another. He rose and climbed the stairs to bid his mother good night. He held her hand and listened to the rattle of her breathing, then realised he had forgotten the sound of her voice; how she talked, how gentle or coarse her words and what familiar names she called him by. He wiped away a tear of remorse. Then he kissed her and snuffed out the lamp.

As he left his mother's room he realised the tambour clock upon her mantle had resumed its ticking.

He walked downstairs, but the young woman had already gone.

◄—●—►

She came mostly in the early evening, without even the sound of a door being opened – as if she'd stepped from the shadows in the corners of the room. Billy knew that his mother's tambour clock was old and that summer was approaching, yet whenever the young woman came to visit, the clock stopped and twilight seemed to hang in the air forever. She was a good teacher, patient and kind. She schooled him in the alphabet and brought him gifts – paper, books, a pen-knife, ink and quills. She taught him the magic of numbers too – to count, and then to multiply, subtract and divide. Billy's mind had always been quick and he worked hard, partly to better himself, but mostly to win his teacher's smile. She taught him how to tend the walled garden. There was more than enough food now, so Billy sold eggs and vegetables from a basket outside the Moon and Sixpence, or at the church gate on weekdays. Soon, he bought another hen, and another. At night, in his bed, he told Cloudfoot of the tall, beautiful woman who brought light, warmth, and laughter back into the Tresize home.

But sorrow often follows in the footsteps of joy.

Billy had long harboured the suspicion that keeping Cloudfoot was against Nature. She was recovered now and it was selfish, he concluded, to hold a wild animal in such captivity. She was not a hen to be kept in a cage. She was made for speed, to stretch her long legs and become a white blur across the moors and open country. So he constructed a simple cage from fruit boxes and, with a heavy heart, carried her back to the barrows of Caer Bran.

The day was warm as Billy said goodbye. He placed the rough-made cage on the spot he'd found her and hoped she would remember the way back to her home in the thicket. He spoke to her and thanked her for her affection and companionship; he hoped she would always remember him, as he would remember her. He wished her a long life, that she would meet a noble buck-hare and raise a fine family of leverets. He hoped that she would always remain happy and safe. Then he opened the cage and lifted her out.

Cloudfoot sat on the grass and tested the breeze with a cautious nose. One ruby eye shone in Billy's direction. There seemed to be a question in it. Billy stood, picked up the cage and backed away. Cloudfoot did not move. He turned his back and walked down from the barrows.

When he glanced behind, Cloudfoot was still there, watching him. He walked some more, then stopped and looked again. She was gone.

Billy kicked stones and clods of earth from the ground, and struck the wooden cage against the stile at the St. Just Road. He wiped his sleeve across his eyes and tried to temper his anger with the knowledge that he had done right. But what of foxes, traps, or guns? He was worried for her now. At home he threw the cage into the garden, kicked the mud from his boots and slammed the door. Then, in an instant, his heart was made whole again.

There, in the middle of the parlour floor, one bright eye upon him, sat Cloudfoot.

'Why, how fast you are!' he declared and scooped her up. There would be no peelings or bean casings for her that night. He fed her fresh carrots and spinach. He'd done his part, he thought. He'd given her back. But Cloudfoot had made up her own mind on the matter.

The evenings grew longer still and Billy was glad to find his lessons did the same. When he demonstrated good progress in spelling and arithmetic, his teacher rewarded him with schooling of a less serious nature. She taught him checkers and then to play cards, a simple game of *wagers* first. They played for beans and buttons.

Billy told her how Cloudfoot had returned from Caer Bran after he'd set her free. He wondered if Cloudfoot had grown too tame, too used to comfort.

Billy's teacher sorted the cards in her hand. 'Or perhaps she feels her business with you is not yet concluded?' she said.

'Not concluded – how?' asked Billy.

'Perhaps she is still to repay you – for the kindness you have shown her?'

It was an explanation Billy liked.

In time, Billy learned to play more challenging card games. He learned of *euchre,* of the *benny* and the *bowers*. It was a game much favoured in the district, a game for four players in teams of two. So Billy learned to play it with his teacher double-handed, or *ghost-handed* as she called it.

One night their game concluded as Billy scraped the last of the buttons and beans towards him. His mistress sulked playfully and begged another round.

'But you have no stake to play with,' Billy observed.

'You could lend it me,' she offered with a smile.

'But I shall not,' replied Billy.

'Then against all I have lost tonight – I'll wager you a kiss,' she said.

Billy was quick to accept and played in earnest. But she trumped him soundly and the wager went unpaid.

That night she read to him. She read him tales of sea-wet cliffs and smugglers' moons, of cutlass, compass, and cannon. He saw the words rise in her soft throat, but he never heard them. Instead, he watched the movement of her lips and dreamt he'd won at cards.

One evening after lessons, her eyes burned bright. 'Tell me, Billy Tresize, what is it you wish for more than anything in the world? And tell me the thing you really *want*, not the one you think you *should*.'

Billy's eyes lingered on her then lifted to the upstairs room. 'I wish my mother to be as once she was,' he said.

A frown darkened her face, but a smile soon chased it away. 'You are a kind soul and a dutiful son,' she said. 'And, in time, you will be a better man than most.' She patted her apron and looked about, speaking cheerfully, 'Is there strong drink or liquor in this house?'

'There is lovage in the pantry and madeira for cooking, I think,' answered Billy.

'Go fetch it,' she said.

Billy found the madeira and brought it to the parlour table. She poured measures into two small glasses and offered him one. Billy brought it to his nose. It smelled sweet and forbidden. She held her own glass aloft and bade him do the same. Then she poured the greater portion of the drink across the floor and said, 'For the god of the place.' Her eyes fell upon Billy, exhorting him to do likewise. He spilled his drink saying, 'For the god of the place.' Then they drank. The liquor was smooth in his mouth, but it burned down to his stomach. He coughed while she laughed.

Billy had no idea what he had done and he never asked. He thought it some kind of game, a joke at the expense of custom. Then, before the week was out, the rattle left his mother's throat and bloodspots no longer marked her pillow. In the weeks that followed, the sores which covered her face and hands became dry skin and fell away. Her breathing eased and the tremors left her. She slept deeply. When she was close to wakefulness Billy found it easier to feed her. Her appetite was returning but her gaze wandered the room and her speech was soft beyond hearing. Billy sat with her for longer now. He told her of recent events, how the garden flourished, how summer had come. He picked her wild flowers from the hedgerows and read to her from books. The geometry of his life seemed complete in its design now. It was a triform knot that tied together the three things most dear to him: Cloudfoot, his recovering mother, and his teacher. It was the happiest Billy had ever been.

◄—•—►

Time makes pretty paintings of our memories. It takes license with ugliness and creates perfection where there was none. Darker aspects are washed over in bright colours. Time is an unreliable curator, and the gallery of our memories is hung with many falsehoods.

So it was with Billy and the memory of his mother.

He was reading to her one afternoon when he saw her eyes upon him.

'When did you learn to read?' she asked, her voice clear.

'I have a teacher now,' he said.

'You do not work?'

'I have been tending you.'

'Then how have we made ends meet?'

'The Women's Mission.'

She fixed him with a stormy look. 'Are we paupers yet?'

He shook his head.

'Then do not open the door to them again. I will have no charity.' She looked towards the open casement and the bright day outside. 'And who pays your teacher?'

'No one.'

'Then your teacher's bill is settled. The job is done. And you must return to the mine.'

Once more, Billy rose before dawn to meet the captain's wagon. The ponies remembered him and pressed around, nosing his pockets in search of treats. His mother was still too weak to rise, so, at night, he brought her supper then sat in the parlour, exhausted, with Cloudfoot in his lap. The young woman came less often now. Sometimes, when he missed her most, she was already beside him – as if his wish had charmed her into being. When she came, they merely smiled and did not speak until Billy's mother was asleep. Then, leaning close, their discourse was whispered into each other's ears. So were the stories she continued to read him. Her closeness and her breath upon his ear gave enchantment to their secrecy. For Billy, it was madeira – sweet and forbidden. Billy's mother grew in strength till one day she dressed herself and came downstairs.

And discord came with her.

She seemed to place no moment on the period of her infirmity. She scrubbed it out like a stain on a floorboard. She asked no questions, gave no thanks. She hung in the house like a fog, and Billy felt its coldness upon him.

She took offence to Cloudfoot and forbade the animal inside. Billy pleaded, but she was unmoved. Had he not earned this one small privilege? Had he not wished his mother's recovery? Had he not wished to see her happy? Why could she not do the same for him? He made a place for Cloudfoot in the chicken coop but the hens fussed and pecked her. In the evenings he took her from the coop and sat with her in the walled garden.

His mother also rebuked him for bringing in so small a wage. It was not enough, she said, and browbeat him into extra shifts. She herself, through lack of strength, could no longer wear the bal-maiden's bonnet and apron. Her answer was to rent Billy's room.

Billy was given a cot in the draughty passageway outside the parlour. He felt temporary; an unpacked box left in a hall, waiting for the day someone might find him a home.

They took in a lodger named Bolitho. He had no trade as such, and did whatever came his way; honest work or questionable. Billy's mother said Bolitho was a *man with prospects*. The cold fog lifted in Bolitho's presence and untrustworthy rays of sunshine could be seen.

Billy knew he was just a chancer. Bolitho had a dog too, a bull terrier of dangerous disposition. It chewed the furniture, slept in Bolitho's room and made more of a home for itself in the house than Billy or Cloudfoot.

Within weeks Bolitho ran up his true colours. He arrived home one evening from an ale-house. His collar was torn and his eye was closed from bruising. He'd been beaten.

'Thieves!' he cried, as he eased himself into a chair. The only thing stolen from him was a precious deck of French playing cards. He had been robbed of nothing more. The cards were marked.

'What did they take?' asked Billy.

'My cards,' complained Bolitho, nursing his cheek.

'You may borrow mine,' offered Billy.

The hand fell from Bolitho's face. 'You have cards?'

'I do.'

'Can you use them?'

'I can.'

'What do you play?'

'Euchre, mostly.'

Bolitho crossed the room and cleared the parlour table. 'Show me,' he said.

They played two-handed until supper and Bolitho failed to win a single trick. He seemed to forget his injuries and became rapt with the boy's ability. After supper they played some more. Billy protested he was tired. Bolitho, after every hand he lost, pressed Billy into another. He watched closely, looking to uncover a technique, a method, a trick, but saw none.

'It's just luck,' said Bolitho, shuffling. 'Just pure, dumb, god-given luck!'

'But from which god?' asked Billy's mother, stacking plates in the kitchen dresser.

'Who cares?' said Bolitho, a smile further disfiguring his face. 'Perhaps we have no need of French decks, eh? Perhaps I have found a new partner.' He lolled in his chair. 'I think the boy should join me at the Moon and Sixpence this Friday. Let's see how deep his luck really runs.'

⬩

Billy trudged to the Moon and Sixpence after his shift and met Bolitho at the appointed time. Many of the players protested at a boy sitting as his partner, but Bolitho made it plain it was his own money on the table and asked if they objected to the winning of it.

The players relented and Billy was dealt in. Bolitho pushed the ante high to start, betting that the opposing team would seek to take advantage of a mere boy. His ploy succeeded and the cards fell his way. By nightfall, Bolitho had emptied the pockets of every player in the tavern and filled himself with brandy in the balance.

Despite Billy's commitments at the mine, his exhaustion, and aversion to the venture in general, he found himself dragged to the taverns of the surrounding towns.

Bolitho was amazed at the prodigious gifts of his young partner. Billy could trounce an opposing team even while his eyes were closing. Bolitho's strategy that Billy might be regarded as an unseasoned player and an easy conquest attracted plenty of fresh pockets to empty. At each and every game they stripped hardworking men of hard-won wages.

Then came the whispers, the mutterings. Men in the public houses stroked their moustaches in suspicion. Others narrowed their eyes above the glowing bowls of their clay pipes. In St. Just one day as Billy finished work, a woman with her ragged brood in tow screamed accusations from across the street. A man spat at his boots.

Billy complained to his mother. He was being relied upon for the entire income of the house: both from the mine and from the gambling. He was too tired now for the wet ladders and gantries of the mine. It was becoming dangerous. He wanted the gambling to stop.

'Until you earn a man's wage and not a boy's, you will do as I say,' said his mother. Like Bolitho, she had grown accustomed to his success at the euchre table.

Billy spoke plainly then, he wanted no part in the ruin of

honest folk. His mother called him ungrateful and beat him until she was breathless.

He slept a few hours and woke before dawn to meet the captain's wagon. While Bolitho and his mother slept upstairs, he splashed his face with cold water and studied his reflection in the dark window. The boy who stared back at him was pale and empty. He looked through the window to the walled garden beyond. She stood at its centre, watching him. Her smile knew his pain.

He threw open the door and flew into her arms. She smoothed his hair and rested her chin on top his head. He told her of the twisted track his life now followed; a track he felt would only lead to penury and damnation. He looked up to see the profile of her face, and a single, sidelong eye. 'I made the wrong wish,' he confided, feeling the words catch in his gullet.

'Because you made the wish you thought you *should*,' she said. 'That makes you kind. It means you think of others first.' She placed a finger on his chest. 'But, what's in here? What do you *really* wish?'

'That one day, I might marry...' he said, '...and to a bride like you.'

Her smile was bright. 'Do you remember your arithmetic?'

'I do.'

'Then tell me, what is three, times three, times three?'

Billy studied his hand. The fingers folded and unfolded. He looked up. 'Twenty-seven,' he said.

Dawn's first light set her eye ablaze. 'Then, on your twenty-seventh birthday, which I know to be the third day of the third month – wait outside Sancreed Church at three in the afternoon, and your bride will appear.'

'Is this another wish?' asked Billy.

'No,' she said. 'It is a promise.'

———◆———

'He's losing on purpose,' said Bolitho one evening from his seat at the parlour table. His dog was at his feet, licking itself.

Billy's mother slapped the knife she held onto the chopping board. 'Is this true?' she asked without turning.

'My luck is running thin,' said Billy. His voice lacked conviction.

'He lies,' said Bolitho.

'You do not know that,' said Billy.

'I see your discards. I see the order in which you play the trumps. Do you think me a fool?'

'No...' began Billy.

'His luck still holds,' announced Bolitho.

His mother indicated the iron cooking pot with the point of the knife. 'We only eat turnip and potatoes tonight,' she said, 'because you lose at cards, and for no good reason.'

'Is it my job to support this house wholly?' asked Billy.

'If you have the talent, then yes!' shouted his mother.

'The boy needs bringing round,' said Bolitho, 'and I know the lesson for it.' He rose and walked into the walled garden.

'*He* could drink less brandy,' said Billy, pointing to Bolitho's vacant chair. 'Then he could cover his rent fairly, without my aid.'

Bolitho reappeared swinging Cloudfoot by the ears. 'Nothing for the pot you say? I say the boy must pay his way and we'll eat meat tonight.'

Billy was upon Bolitho in an instant, tears of fury sprang to his eyes. He wrestled to free Cloudfoot while Bolitho's dog snapped at the dangling hare. Bolitho lifted Cloudfoot above the reach of both, cursing. So Billy wound back his arm and struck him under the ribs. His mother screamed. Bolitho reeled, dropping Cloudfoot to the savagery of the dog. Bolitho's reply was to wind back his own arm and strike Billy in return. Billy went to the ground, but fear brought him quickly to his feet. The dog seized Cloudfoot in its jaws and began to shake the life from her. Billy took a fire-iron from beside the range and brought it down across the dog's back, once, twice. The third time he brought it down hard. The dog turned on Billy now, tugging and tearing at a trouser-leg. Cloudfoot hobbled to the still-open door and out into the garden. The dog gave up on Billy's trouser and gave chase. Bolitho had left the chicken coop open, too. Cloudfoot, from habit, sought sanctuary inside the coop, but the dog was already upon her. It ran inside and, in its frenzy, killed the indignant hen and murdered one of her companions. Billy caught the dog by the hind legs and pulled it out before it savaged Cloudfoot once more. The dog turned and this time bit through Billy's hand, holding tight. Billy cried out in pain, but let the dog pull and tug while he watched Cloudfoot limp to the iron gate and slip between its bars. The dog saw the ploy. It released Billy and turned in pursuit, but was stopped by the gate. It barked and barked after Cloudfoot. Through the bars Billy watched her – a bleeding, white shape, hopping with faltering stride across the fields beyond.

Behind him, Bolitho stood at the back door. 'It'll be turnip and tatties tonight then,' he grumbled.

From the back of the wagon, Billy watched the pre-dawn darkness swallow the simple, hard, ungracious house. He nursed his bandaged hand and swore never to return. He knew now that people who were cruel to animals would always be cruel to people too.

He slept the first two nights in the stable with the ponies. In the day he went to the count house and begged an advance on wages, then asked about for lodgings he could afford. A family in Pendeen who'd lost a son to the mine took him in. He slept in the bed between the dead boy's sister and brother. As he grew, so did his wage. In time, he rented a single room of his own. At last, he felt he'd earned the right to take up space in this world. He became tall. His gentle expression and the roof-tile red of his hair turned the bonnet of many a young bal-maiden. Sometimes he smiled back, but that was the end of it.

He became known as an able *charge-man*. The goose-quill fuses were treacherous and prone to misfire. They claimed limbs and lives, but not when Billy trimmed and set them. He had a way with them. His fellows dubbed him *Lucky Bill*, and welcomed him most gladly when he worked the same seam.

The entrances to Botallack mine were in the high cliffs overlooking the sea. The engine-houses that drove the pumps and winches clung to the same rock as the gulls and gannets. Inside the mine a steep incline led down to the vertical shafts which plummeted below sea-level, then followed the tin lodes out under the sea.

Botallack was home to one of the deepest shafts in the world. So deep, it was told, that you could hear the picks and shovels of the damned working underfoot. The miners called it *The Devil's Chimney*. Whenever the men stopped work at the end of its furthest tunnels, they could hear the thunder of the sea above them moving great boulders across the ocean floor.

Here, two hundred fathoms deep and nearly a mile out to sea, Billy was at work when the Disaster of the Devil's Chimney took place. Consistent with other events in his life, it occurred just three days before his twenty-seventh birthday.

Looking back, to call the event a disaster would pull the truth too thin. The disaster was only a financial one for the mine.

The cause was nothing underground, either. The accident happened on the surface. A boiler in one of the great beam engines spat a rivet and began to tear itself open. The engineers braced it with timber and filled its belly with Welsh coal to keep the pressure up, but the pumps that drew the seawater from the mine began to fail.

By good fortune, these events unfolded just on the change of shift. The mine captains had the wherewithal to stop fresh teams descending while the outgoing shift was already making its way to the surface. The order was shouted down to clear the mine. Billy knew something was wrong before word even reached his ears. The lower galleries had begun to flood and the men were running for the shaft-ladders. Crouched low, Billy hurried through the dark tunnels until his lamp picked out bright eyes watching him. The ponies stood, still harnessed to the ore-carts, waiting to be drowned.

'Lend a hand!' shouted Billy at the men fighting each other for a foothold on the ladder. No one joined him. Billy unhitched the carts as the water rose to his knees, then waded through the nearby galleries in search of any remaining ponies. He chased them to the skip shaft. He had a thought that the animals could still be winched by their girth straps up to the incline shaft. He shouted up the ladders to several lamplit figures far above. 'Hey! Man the skip-whim and help me pull the ponies out!'

'You will die trying,' someone shouted down. 'Climb the ladder and leave them!'

'There's time yet. I will stay to hitch them. You work the whim!' The figures above seemed to conspire, then turned for the ladders once more. Billy screamed out their names, pointing. 'I know you, I know you all. And here I stay until the last of these creatures is winched out. If you will not aid me, then you shall be known as the men who left Lucky Bill to die!'

There was another round of conspiracy, then one of the figures separated from the group. In a moment, Billy heard the operation of the skip-whim. He hitched the frightened animals and watched them rise. Once on the incline shaft, the ponies had to be chased up and out the mine. It was a direction unfamiliar to them. They emerged in daylight and ran, terrified, through Botallack town. Some found refuge in the shadows between houses, others would not be calmed until coal sacks were pulled over their heads. The water was up to Billy's chest as he struggled to hitch the last of the ponies, an old dappled mare he'd known from his youth. He'd named her Appleseed. There came the sound of breaking timber, then a surge of seawater hit them, carrying them away from the foot of the shaft into roaring tunnels of darkness. Billy gripped Appleseed's bridle. He collided with something – a ladder rising up into an overhand stope, a cavern above them dug by men in quest of precious ore. The rush of water lifted them up. Billy guessed the stope was holding air. He clung to the ladder, and to the frightened, snorting pony as she trod water. They hung there for an eternity. Billy fastened his belt to the ladder. In his grasp he felt the old mare fight bravely to stay afloat. He closed his eyes. When he opened them, his hand was empty.

He had a notion that days were passing, then only hours. He thought himself at home in bed, recovering. He pictured Appleseed floating, suspended in dark water. He left the mine so many times in his mind and walked in sunlight to Sancreed. He saw the bright, sidelong eye burn and watched her lips. 'Wake up,' she whispered in his ear.

When Billy awoke, he was hanging from the ladder in damp air, his back painfully arched. He heard the beautiful sound of the seawater pumps and laughed a wretched laugh. With cold, aching limbs he climbed down and felt his way through the adits to the ladder-shaft. And on the third day, to Billy's reckoning, he ascended the Devil's Chimney into light.

In the brightness of the day, men he could not see clapped his back and shook his hand. 'What time is it?' he asked with a deathbed voice. Someone hugged him. 'What time is it?' he asked again.

A man leaned close, a mine captain in jacket and tie. 'Nearly two in the afternoon, why so?'

Billy spun the man around, pulling off his jacket. 'Now lend me your tie,' Billy pressed.

The mine captain laughed and pulled it over his head. 'Gladly, for Lucky Bill,' he said.

As his eyes became accustomed to the burning light, Billy ran. He ran through Botallack and struck across the moors. With ragged breath he fell onto the St. Just Road and ran along it towards Sancreed, pulling his arms through the mine captain's jacket. He wound the tie around his neck and made the path outside Sancreed church at just after three.

His wild eyes pierced me through the mud and dirt on his face. 'Boy, was there a woman here just now?' he asked.

'No, sir,' I said (for in truth I had not seen any).

He walked away from me then back again. 'What time is it?' he asked.

I found his question strange because the bell-tower had just sounded. 'Just after three,' I replied.

'And there was no lady here before?'

'No, sir.'

'And you have been here long?'

'A half-hour to sweep the path.' I held up my broom.

'Then I shall wait,' he watched the gate with hands upon his waist as I resumed my sweeping. As the minutes passed, he began to slump. His head hung. 'What day is it?' he asked in solemn tone.

'Wednesday, sir.'

'What date?'

'Why sir, the fourth.'

He looked at me, as if run through with a mortal wound. Then he marched up and down the path. He beat his breast, he pulled his ears, he shouted curses at the sky, then came to a halt before me.

'Were you here yesterday?' he asked.

'I was.'

'At what time?'

'The same time.'

'And was there a lady here then?' he asked.

'No lady,' I returned.

His brows gathered. 'Then who?'

'Only a hare. A white hare with eyes of flame. It sat on the path and watched the gate,' I said.

His eyes began to flood then, like seawater through a mine.

— ● —

My account was true. Just the day before I had come to sweep when I found the hare sitting in the middle of the path, bold as sin, with eyes to the gate. The bell had just struck three. I scolded the animal and pushed it with my broom. It moved, but paid little heed. So I swept it briskly from the path. The animal made a circle and came back to sit where it had been. It was then I heard my name hissed from behind. I turned to see Jeb, the old sexton, beckoning me from his place of concealment near the corner of the church.

'Leave it be, leave it be,' said Jeb in a flap of consternation. 'Do you know what that *is*?'

I crouched beside him, watching the hare between the headstones. 'No.'

''Tis a *witch-hare*,' he whispered in dire tone.

'A witch?'

'Aye, some who take the shape are in league with the Dark One, old *Bucca-Dhu* himself.' He leaned so close that I saw the lacework of veins at the end of his nose. 'But some are *pellars* too, white witches who serve the light.'

'So which is this?' I asked, afraid.

'There is no way of knowing,' he said. 'So prudence be the best recourse. If anyone has need of me, they may find me at the Moon and Sixpence.' He made to leave, then turned to me again. 'And to avoid a curse, go home and tear up your clothes before coming here again.'

I did as Old Jeb advised. Once home, I tore up my shirt and trousers. It vexed my mother so. She chased me round the house and thrashed me with a wooden spoon.

A savage fever, brought on by his privations, then took hold of Billy. He hung between death and consciousness for days, raving in delirium. Years later, he told me of his experience.

He dreamt he'd left his bed and walked to Caer Bran. It was not night or day, but something of both, and the landscape glimmered in the spectral light. He climbed the hill and found it lit about with points of brightness like spriggans' lamps that danced, colourful and mercurial, in the magic-charged air.

Set into the hill he saw a shimmering gate which opened at his approach. Stepping through, he followed a bejewelled staircase deep inside the earth, down to a great hall where a beautiful queen with a wounded arm sat weeping on a throne of glass.

He returned to health, but the gentle smile was no longer with him.

His words now were few. To distance himself from sorrow, he took a ship to America and joined the Colorado Gold Rush. Although he had lost so much, he never lost his luck, especially in matters of pick, fuse, and charge. Later, he left America a rich man and burned his neck in the opal fields of Australia. There, too, his good fortune was currency he could count on. He became a man of great wealth and even opened his own mining company.

Memories came to him then, faint and distant, like snatches of a melody hummed by a woman he once knew. He remembered the honeysuckle smell of gorse-flower and the salt sting of the Atlantic wind. He longed for them, and they brought him home again to Sancreed.

The flame of red that was once his hair had burned out, leaving only the whiteness of ash. He was an old man now, and his eyes still carried their old sorrow.

He purchased a large farmhouse near Caer Bran and a broad swathe of countryside around it. People gossiped that his brain was addled. What could he want with it? He was no farmer. He called upon me to be his steward and gamekeeper. The wage was more than fair and the work was light, yet the title of my engagement perplexed me for there was no game at Caer Bran and he would never hunt. In time, the fullness of his plan revealed itself.

He became concerned with gates. He wanted to secure his land. But he had no cattle and never rented to tenant farmers. I saw no reason. He engaged a blacksmith in Madron to fabricate tall gates of metal at a time when steel and iron were scarce. 'I'll get you steel and iron,' Billy told the smithy.

I helped him hitch a pair of horses to a sprung cart and together we travelled. First, we visited the ironmongers, saddleries and gun-smiths of the neighbouring towns. Billy bought every animal trap there was for sale – leg-holds, coil-springs and snares; pole-traps, evil-looking long-springs and vicious, toothed gins. He took delight in the exercise and became filled with a boyish mischief. We travelled as far as Okehampton and denied every farmer, sportsman and poacher in the county a way to maim animals. Billy delivered the steel traps to the smithy and told him not to beautify his work. Soon the *Trap-Gates* were hung – great monstrosities gaping with iron jaws and teeth. They were as much to keep people out as animals in, said Billy, and they made it plain to all who saw them that there would be no traps set on the land of Billy Tresize.

News of this escapade spread, drawing anger from many, but also allegiance from those who felt the same. Billy was petitioned by all manner of society, club, association and charity whose charter it was to protect innocent creatures from the harm wrought by Man. Billy obliged in every way he could. He lent voice to the lobbyists and made generous donations. Their fight became his own.

The land inside the Trap-Gates was offered to all animals in need of protection. The *Caer Bran Sanctuary* Billy called it. First, he saved old pit-ponies from the knacker's knife. Hardy little souls they were, frightened at first by birdsong and the vastness of the sky above. Next came the retired brewer's drays and draught horses – gentle giants with bearded hooves. Then the badger dug his set, the shriek-owl made her nest, and so came the skylark, lapwing and chough. The voles and field mice brought the falcons and the stoat. Then rabbits by the score made their warrens there.

But not one hare came back to Caer Bran.

The last time I saw Billy Tresize in the world was during one of our walks along the St. Just Road. He stopped where the road skirts the moor and lifted his eyes to Caer Bran. The weather was hung with clouds and the summit lay hidden. Billy's eyes were veiled with mist in sympathy with the weather.

'Do you think me lucky, Tom?' he asked.

'I know there's not a man in the county who'd sit at a card table with Billy Tresize,' I said, laughing.

He made no laugh in return, but kept his eyes upon the shrouded hilltop.

'They say you are the luckiest man in the world,' I added.

His chin began to tremble then. 'And so I might have been,' he said, 'but for the loss of just one day.'

He died at the close of the month. Three days before his birthday.

◄ ● ►

The little girl beside me has given up on the spring lamb. It wanders the church, bleating for its dam. From the pulpit I hear the droning of Father Jessop. And my mind wanders too.

Three, times three, times three.

The numbers still hold me. Most certain, they total twenty-seven by the usual reckoning. But is there another, hidden total, arrived at by more unusual calculation?

What if the numbers are not merely multiplied by three, but *each by the other?*

For three times three is nine, and nine times nine is...

I feel my mother's wooden spoon strike the back of my neck

from beyond the grave.

...Eighty-one.

And would today not be Billy's eighty-first birthday?

I pull my watch from a pocket and open the cover. The hands swing to three o'clock and then no further. I wind the crown-spindle, tap the glass and hold it to my ear.

So consumed am I by the stopping of my pocket-watch that I almost fail to hear the grinding of the hinges to the South Door. She steps past me now, for I know it is her. She is tall, long-limbed and youthful still; more fair than even Billy had described. As she passes the fractious animals, they become calm and look to her in silence. So do the people of the congregation. Only Father Jessop, too in love with the sound of his eulogy, continues reading from the pulpit. Then, he too sees her, and his mouth falls open like an oven door.

To the consternation of all, she steps up to Billy's casket and lifts the lid. She smooths his brow and strokes his cheek. Then, causing the ladies in the front pews to gasp with horror, she bends low and places such a long and tender kiss upon Billy's lips as would make old Bucca-Dhu blush.

She straightens, draws down the lid and steps from the chancel. But in her face I see no trace of grief, no sorrow, or regret. Only a smile, small and bright, like the sun peeping over a window-sill.

Back along the aisle she walks, briskly now, towards the South Door, and all the while her smile grows. Then she claps her hands, she laughs for joy, and breaks into a run.

And can she run. (Did I not tell you that her legs are long and made for speed?)

She shoots past me. The hymn sheets fly, the candles gutter.

I rise with joints made stiff by kneeling in prayer and stand to watch the South Door.

But it is no woman I see run from Sancreed Church.

In her stead I see *two shapes*: the forms of two hares; one cloud-white, the other as red as a roof-tile. Together they jump the lychgate and the hedge beyond. Then, as one, they race across the open country, gambolling in the sunshine, straight towards the barrows of Caer Bran.

A Thank-You

If you enjoyed this book, you can help other readers find my work by leaving an online review with the retailer you purchased it from, or at Goodreads.

Many thanks,

Jeff

About These Stories

THE FINAL STORY in this book is the one I wrote first. So I'll begin there. At the end.

The Hare Bride is pivotal because it was the first time I'd written anything historical. I've read many classics from the Victorian and Edwardian era and always wanted to explore a more historical _voice_ with my writing.

The opportunity presented itself in 2021 when a friend and fellow writer, Clare Rhoden, asked if I'd like to contribute a story to an upcoming anthology. Clare had pitched the idea for this anthology to Black Ink Fiction in the USA and they'd accepted. The anthology was to be titled _Fantasy on Four Feet_ and would contain stories from the natural world, told from the perspective of animals.

My plan was to write a story about the natural witchcraft of the place I was born and raised: Cornwall in the UK. I grew up with many of its myths and legends, particularly the witches of Sancreed, St. Buryan and Zennor. Cornish witches are a singular breed. They've been known to ride brooms but this is often considered too showy, too _look at me_. Instead, when travelling from A to B, they prefer to take the form of Britain's fastest land animal: the hare.

In the wider Celtic tradition (of which Cornwall shares a part), hares are mystical creatures. They are familiars, shapeshifters, tricksters and guardians of the underworld. I wondered what might happen if a witch was trapped in hare form due to injury and then fell in love with her rescuer. I was creeping towards a mythic romance and, in this, took inspiration from the beautiful Irish story of *Oisín and the Hare* (my own version of which is relayed in Billy's dream). The church, the village and the iron-age hilltop fortress of Caer Bran all exist. As do the now-disused tin mines of Botallack Crowns. I've grown up with stories of the tin mines and can claim several *hard rock men* among my forebears. So the landscape, the anecdotes, dialect and myth were already large in my imagination.

I enjoyed writing <u>The Hare Bride</u> so much that I wrote other stories using a similar voice.

<u>Rats' Alley</u> followed, then the others, until lastly I wrote <u>The Leper's Garden</u>. It was then I knew I'd found a title for this collection and a style and flavour that held the whole together.

Directly on the heels (paws, hooves, pads) of *Fantasy on Four Feet*, Clare again contacted me with an idea she'd had while walking her dog. This was to commission an anthology of short stories inspired by T. S. Eliot's *The Waste Land*. The launch would coincide with the centenary of the poem's publication and, while we languished in lockdown, sheltering from a pandemic wasteland of our own, the timing couldn't have been more appropriate. She asked if I'd like to contribute and as a fan of Eliot's work there was no way I could refuse. The poem is a modernist masterpiece written shortly after the Great War and is loaded with many rich thoughts that a writer can use as starting points for a story.

Clare assembled a stellar team of international writers. We each chose a stanza from the poem and developed a story around it. I chose the following:

Speak to me. Why do you never speak. Speak.
What are you thinking of? What thinking? What?
I never know what you are thinking. Think.
   I think we are in rats' alley
Where the dead men lost their bones.

For me, these lines seem a poignant dramatisation of battle-related PTSD. Within the verses we can suppose an exchange is taking place between an ex-soldier and a loved one. The loved one reaches out but can never be part of their companion's world. They remain locked outside, never to experience or understand it. The other, the soldier, occupies the present physically, yet lives forever in the past, haunted by memories of war in the trenches.

That a couple could be intimate, yet divided; together, yet apart, is a heartbreaking thought and one I wished to explore. For sufferers, trauma also blurs boundaries between past and present, the everyday and the terrifying. This combination of ideas led me naturally in the direction of a romantic horror story.

And so, _Rats' Alley_ came into being. It formed part of Clare's excellent anthology and even made the finals of the Aurealis Awards as best horror novella of 2023.

The end-game that plays out in Rats' Alley is put together from factual accounts. Soldiers did write last letters to loved ones and prayers for deliverance, pinning them to the trench wall. Would I have done the same? Would I have prayed to a God who appeared not to care? Who appeared absent? Or would I have prayed to a darker god who might just be willing to listen?

The Songbird on Sampan Street is an ode to one of the places I love best in the world: the city of Hong Kong. It's also a testament to the friendliness and resilience of its wonderful people. Hong Kong is a place that gets under your skin and never quite leaves you: an intoxicating collision of east and west, of culture, language and cuisine. I've lived there twice, the first time during the 1980s while the city and territories were a British Colony. The second time was from 2006 to 2011 while Hong Kong was a Special Administrative Region of the People's Republic of China. I speak a smattering of Cantonese, so the romanised translations are my own.

Sampan Street exists. Like Philby, the English protagonist in the story, I sometimes walked along Sampan Street on my way to work. The location is also accurate in that the Wanchai Flower Market used to be situated nearby. I've always loved the street's name and often wondered as to its origin. As you may know, a _sampan_ is a small, flat-bottomed boat, the deck of which is traditionally made with three long planks of timber. In Cantonese, 'sam pan' means 'three planks'. Hence the name. Today the street is nowhere near the harbour and it's doubtful that even centuries ago, before the foreshore was extensively reclaimed, that it ever was. Perhaps it was a place where the vessels were constructed? Perhaps it was once a canal? Perhaps there was a makeshift bridge of three planks? I don't know, and I don't really need an answer. Isn't that the way some things should stay? Questions stir the imagination and evoke wonder. I like that. I like mysteries. That's why I've always loved Sampan Street.

The story alternates between the first person as an inner monologue and the third person as a narrative account. I found this mix of perspectives a great way to tell two sides of the same story: the outer, extant story being the language-less friendship of Philby and Choi, and the inner story being the grief that Philby hides from the world. There is no language that can adequately express grief. It's personal. It's silent. It's a collapsing inwards. That's why I wanted Philby and Choi to understand each other through empathy, not words.

But is it a work of dark fiction? It's a story about loss and the meaning of happiness. It explores a belief within many cultures that the souls of the departed are taken from us in the form of birds. But is the supernatural genuinely at work here? It might be. It might not. I prefer to leave that decision to you, the reader.

This is also why I've sometimes struggled to understand where my writing *fits*. I don't always write from the centre of the dark fiction genre or observe its conventions, although I'm envious of the writers who can. It's just not how the stories come to me. My work is often more optimistic, more hopeful. The lighter end of dark fiction.

I was wondering how to lead my storytelling back to the darkness when the idea for <u>The Deceiver's Tale</u> jaywalked across my line of thinking. I wanted to write a really good horror story and I was trying to understand what that might look like. It occurred to me that great horror is like a trip to the zoo to look at crocodiles, lions or Kodiak bears through glass. You're staring at beasts that could rip you limb from limb, yet you're in no danger. That's the paradox of horror: looking on death from a position of safety. This is horror's fascination. Its thrill. From another angle I also thought of a good horror story being like a shark cage. It allows you to be immersed in a frightening, alien environment and gaze upon monsters. I wanted to write a story like that. I wanted to place my reader in a shark cage.

Then the thought landed – *what if the cage door was unlatched?* What if, at some point in the story, it swung open, unknown to the reader, and allowed the monsters inside?

What I was imagining was a way to place the reader *within* the story, at the mercy of its terrors, first hand. I was removing the bars and safety glass. I wondered if I could hide a curse in a story somehow, a curse for the reader that would not become plain until it was too late.

So I began work on <u>The Deceiver's Tale</u>. I chose to conceal the curse by presenting it to the reader in an unfamiliar language and breaking it down, line by line, across larger sections of narrative. In the story, Duranzo's curse would never be read as a whole. So here it is at last, in Spanish and English:

En los nombres de mi Señor y Maestro, el Diablo:
Lucifer, Abaddon, el Padre de la Mentira.
Y en el nombre de sus fieles príncipes:
Baphomet, Astaroth, Amodeus, y todos los cardenales del infierno.
Pongo maldición en esta página:
Que aquellos que lo lean, se les arrancaran las almas,

Y les retendrá aquí,
Como caracteres escritos, protagonistas en una historia propia
de ellos mismos.
A sufrir en la oscuridad y de la soledad,
Para toda la eternidad.

In the name of my Lord and Master, the Devil:
Lucifer, Abaddon, the Father of Lies.
And in the names of his faithful princes:
Baphomet, Astaroth, Amodeus, and all the Cardinals of Hell.
I place a curse upon this page:
That all who read may have their souls plucked out,
And be held captive here,
Written as characters, players in a story of their own,
To suffer in darkness and solitude,
For all eternity.

Here, I owe a special debt of gratitude to Lino Pérez Fernandez for supplying the Spanish version of Duranzo's curse as above. I understand that Lino kept his fingers crossed while working on the translation. I hear he's doing fine. God bless and many thanks to you, Lino.

Many readers have told me that the seafaring nature of the story reminded them of works by C.S. Forester, Herman Melville and even Robert Louis Stevenson. Truth is, it's heavily inspired by the nautical works of Joseph Conrad: *Nostromo*, *Almayer's Folly* and the seminal *Heart of Darkness* – all stories that I've read and loved since I was young.

On the subject of influence, I should also point out that _Pegger Moe_ and _Lazlo the Unformed_ are partly inspired by the short stories of the Pulitzer Prize winner, Steven Millhauser. I adore Millhauser's work. I tend to read his stories once, for pure delight, then a second time to see how he conjured the magic. I first came to his work through _Eisenheim the Illusionist_. His works _In the Penny Arcade_, _The Barnum Museum_ and _The Knife Thrower and Other Stories_ all explore the arcane world of picture halls, sideshows, circuses and funfairs. Entering his stories is a recall to childhood and to believe once again that crossing the threshold of such places is a step into the unknown. His stories make me remember my own visits to such places as a boy: slinking past the boxing tent, too frightened to look up at the battered pugilists calling to the crowd. I also remember my own dismay at paying to view a two-headed horse, only to discover it was an embryo preserved in formaldehyde.

The Forever Child is a tribute too. I wrote it when I learned of the passing of Anne Rice. Although I've always loved the lush, historical gore of her vampire stories I've never been tempted to emulate her. I'd only embarrass myself. So this is perhaps the only vampire story I'll ever write. It started out as an exercise in writing a story in the second person and ended up as a way to give thanks to a wonderful writer.

The Storytellers was first accepted for publication in the anthology _New Tales of Old Volume II – Wolves Among Us_ in 2021 by Gemma Paul and Kate Campbell at Raven & Drake in the UK. Unfortunately, that excellent independent publishing house closed its doors before the book was published. But Gemma made sure the stories would live on, and rescue came in the form of Brandi Hicks and Shelly Jarvis of Black Ink Fiction in the USA who published the anthology. The brief was ingenious: take a well-known wolf story and spin it into something different. My thought was to take one of the most famous fairy tales of all and tell it from the perspective of the wolf. The story is set in the German city of Halle, a place Wilhelm Grimm visited in 1810 to receive treatment for heart and respiratory problems. His brother Jacob remained in Kassel until the printing of *RotKäppchen* (Little Red Riding Hood) in 1812. The zoo, situated on Reilsberg hill, is real but postdates Wilhelm's arrival in Halle. A pity. I would like to think he may have walked there at some time, and perhaps been told a story by a wolf.

In 2023, Black Ink Fiction published another of my stories in *Penny Blood Tales*, an anthology also devised by Gemma Paul. This was to be a homage to the Penny Dreadfuls of the English Victorian era. I'd recently taken a walk through London's Whitechapel area with my youngest daughter and a dear friend from my advertising days. We walked though Spitalfields Market and past The Ten Bells, a pub Jack the Ripper was rumoured to frequent. I pictured the dense, stifling fog of that time and it struck me how impossible it would be to cast a shadow in that world of perpetual haze and gloom. On the same day we visited the Museum of Childhood in nearby Bethnal Green. The museum was crammed with toys from bygone ages and different cultures and I was drawn to the exhibits of Indonesian shadow puppets. As it often works, the two concepts of fog and shadow somehow melded into an idea. *Unshadowed* was the result.

For the longest time I've also admired the writing of Graham Greene. I studied *Brighton Rock* while at school and went on to read

The Heart of the Matter and *The End of the Affair*. Much later I read *Twenty-One Stories* and was delighted to learn that Greene also wrote some magnificent ghost stories. One short story, *The End of the Party*, recounted children playing a game of hide-and-seek, with tragic consequences. It made me think of that childhood desire to hide from the world and to never grow up. To hide away forever. This led me to write my own hide-and-seek story <u>The Hidden</u>. Somewhere along the way it became a love story too.

Finally, to the story that gives its name to this collection, <u>The Leper's Garden</u>.

For some time I wanted to write a revenge story where vengeance is visited upon a wicked or unreliable narrator. I took my cue from an odd piece of urban mythology I heard while living in Hong Kong. The island of Hei Ling Chau forms part of the Hong Kong archipelago and lies just to the south-east of the larger island of Lantau. Today, it's home to a correctional facility and a typhoon shelter for shipping. The island originally bore the name of *Nai Gu Chau*, but was given the name Hei Ling Chau (*Island of Joyful Healing*) when it became a leper colony in 1950. Ignoring the Victorian chronology of my story, this much at least, is fact. The stranger part of the island's story came to me from a friend serving as an officer in the Marine Police. He maintained there was once a restaurant on the island where the wealthy of Hong Kong could dine in safety while watching the lepers outside. It's a thought distasteful enough to put anyone off their food but the idea had an odd whiff of truth about it, especially when considering the proclivities of colonialism. I tried researching this restaurant but found nothing. It's unlikely there was ever such a place. Or, as the voice of conspiracy inside me whispers (and every writer has one), perhaps there *was* such a restaurant, its history wiped clean by an institution too ashamed to admit its existence.

Supposition, conspiracy and intrigue. These should have no place in an ideal world. But to a writer, these are the tools by which fiction is crafted.

And, as a very famous writer once said, *never let the truth get in the way of a good story.*

Jeff Clulow – April 2025

ABOUT THE AUTHOR

Jeff Clulow is a prizewinning author of romantic dark fiction and horror. Born in Cornwall in the UK, Jeff now lives and writes in Sydney, Australia. Jeff's writing leans towards the lighter end of dark fiction, exploring themes of family, childhood, love and loss. He's inspired by folktale, mythology and the notion that old gods still walk among us.

His stories have reached the finals of the Aurealis Awards, the Shadows Awards, the American BookFest Awards and the National Indie Excellence Awards. He has been awarded an 'Honourable Mention' in the Robert N. Stephenson competition for short fiction in horror and is the winner of the 2023 Asylumfest Mayday Hills Ghost Story Competition.

Find out more about Jeff and his work at www.jeffclulow.com

Also by Jeff Clulow

Persephone is a hooker. Hades is a pimp. The goddess Freya is a shopaholic party girl and Thanatos, the Angel of Death, walks the earth as a mild-mannered accountant.

These are the myths you love as you've never experienced them before. Fourteen otherworldly tales of carnage and cruelty, heroism and sacrifice.

Now an award-nominated collection.

Visit the author's website for details.